A *Marriage* *Pact* FOR THE

COWBOY

SWEET RIVER RANCH ROMANCE - BOOK 4

VALERIE COMER

Greenwords Media

O Lord, you have searched me and known me!
Psalm 139:1 ESV

FREE BOOK?

Love cowboys? Me, too! That's why I'd like to offer you an ebook copy of *The Cowboy's Forever Crush* free as an introduction to the world of my Montana Ranches Christian Romance series. This story world encompasses the Saddle Springs series, the Cavanagh Cowboys series, and now the Sweet River Ranch series.

Come on in and be lassoed by love!
https://valeriecomer.com/subscribe-crush

CHAPTER ONE

Maxwell Sullivan hung back in his class reunion's meet-and-greet and scanned the crowd. Who were all these people who seemed to know each other, and why had he come? He hadn't been back to Kansas all that often since graduating from high school ten years ago, much to his mother's dismay.

He shouldn't have come now, either. No one in the teeming gymnasium of Gilead High School would have spared a thought if he wasn't here. Oh, his name might have cropped up in an occasional 'remember when' story, but quite possibly not even that.

"Sullivan? Is that you?" A man with a toddler on his arm stopped in front of him.

"Yes, and you…?" Maxwell scraped his memory down to the bone and couldn't come up with the guy's name. Why hadn't they handed out name tags? Probably because everyone else still knew each other.

"Brandt. Stuart Brandt. Hey, man. It's good to see you.

1

Remember Joanie Thompson? She's around here some-where. I married her, and we have four kids now."

"Oh, yeah? Congrats, Stuart. Good to see you." Not that they'd hung out in the same crowd back then. He remem-bered Joanie, though. Flirty cheerleader. She'd actually settled down?

Maxwell felt old. And very, very single.

Stuart turned. "Reeder! Get over here. Remember Sullivan?"

In minutes, half a dozen guys stood around him. Seemed most of them still lived in Gilead and had married their high school sweethearts.

Stuart turned to Maxwell "What have you been up to?"

Maxwell shrugged. "I spent a few years flipping houses, but I'm living in Montana now, renovating and building cottages at my grandfather's guest ranch."

Garth Reeder blinked. "Your grandfather is a rancher? I thought he was a rich hotel mogul in the Windy City."

The dude didn't have to sound so snarky about it. The other guys didn't need to chuckle. "A guest ranch is a lot like a hotel. Just another business venture in hospitality."

"Montana, huh?" Stuart laughed. "That's a long way from Gilead, Kansas."

In more ways than these guys could ever imagine. Maxwell had wiped the dust of the Plains off his feet and jetted off to Chicago before the ink on his diploma had dried.

There was only one reason he was back in town now. Okay, two.

His mother had begged, cajoled, and coerced him. Maybe Mom was three reasons all by herself.

And he was mildly curious about the Ralston twins: Amelia, in particular. He'd kind of had a thing for her back in the day, not that he'd made a single effort to keep in touch. Too focused. Too busy.

"There's Eryn Ralston now." Stuart jutted his chin toward the door. "Remember her?"

The other twin. The quiet one.

She stood chatting with the person behind the registration table, but she constantly glanced around. How many times had she tucked her long blond hair behind her ear by now? Three? Four? Man, she looked nervous.

Maxwell could relate. He felt as at home in the boardroom as in the midst of a rubble-filled house, but neither was daunting compared to facing the kids he'd known the first 18 years of his life.

"Yeah, I remember Eryn. Is Amelia around somewhere?"

"Oh, man. Didn't you hear?" Stuart's voice lowered ominously.

"Hear what?"

"You know Mrs. Ralston was killed in that accident when we were kids — eighth grade, I think?"

"Yeah?"

"Well, the same thing happened to Amelia in exactly the same intersection."

Maxwell took a step back. "Amelia is *dead*?"

"A couple of years ago now."

"No way." And how had Mom never passed the news on to Maxwell? Maybe she'd forgotten the twins had been in his class. Or maybe she'd finally believed that he didn't care

3

about anyone from back then. "That's awful. How did Eryn take it?"

"Not real well. Her dad isn't doing so great either."

"I can't imagine."

"Yeah, it's been rough for them." Stuart shook his head.

Eryn turned to survey the room and seemed to shrink into herself. Her gaze swept Maxwell without pausing. Maybe she didn't recognize him. He certainly wouldn't have known her anywhere outside of this class reunion in Gilead. Maybe not even here if Stuart hadn't pointed her out.

"I should talk to her." He didn't wait for a reply before skirting the group of guys and heading toward the blonde. "Eryn? I just found out your sister passed away. Please accept my condolences."

She turned and looked at him. "I'm sorry — you are…?"

"Maxwell Sullivan. I remember some Halloween parties and sleigh rides out at your farm when we were kids."

"Max? I wouldn't have recognized you."

"I wouldn't have known you, either." Not a chance. The willowy blonde in front of him barely resembled the awkward girl with braces on her teeth he'd known back then. She'd been shy, too, more focused on studying than dating. No twins could have been less alike.

"Yeah, Amelia's passing… that was a huge shock. It's just Dad and me now." Her smile seemed forced.

"I bet it's been hard." Maxwell knew a bit about that.

"You lost one of your brothers, too."

"I did." Maxwell shook his head, trying to dislodge the memories of discovering his oldest brother and his wife had been killed in a helicopter crash almost two years ago.

Maybe that's why Mom hadn't mentioned Amelia — she'd been too busy mourning her son and taking care of the toddler he'd left behind. "He was seven years older than me, though. We weren't super close. Not like a twin."

Eryn released a shuddering breath. "We had our good and bad moments, of course. We were very different in every way. Still, we were twins, you know?"

"I'm sorry." There wasn't much else to say about that.

"And I was sorry to hear about Wally and his wife. They left a baby, right?"

"Yes, Jamie. My brother Tate and his wife adopted him. He's doing well." It wasn't like a three-year-old could miss the parents he'd spent so little time with.

"That's good. I remember when Tate had a part in the college passion play here — year before last, I think? He was the apostle Peter. Did a great job."

"I flew in for the final performance, and you're right. He was good." Tate was good at everything he did. Made it hard to live up to him, actually. "Funny story. Tate and his wife named their baby Simon Peter. I think Tate wanted to keep reliving his glory days."

"Aw, that's sweet." Eryn smiled. "So, um, I haven't seen you around in like forever."

"I went to work for my grandfather in Chicago right after high school. My dad and my brothers lived there at the time. You?"

She sighed. "I haven't been anywhere at all. I started busing tables at Debby's Diner during high school, and I've moved all the way up to assistant cook."

"Hey, good for you!"

Eryn shook her head. "It's not my dream come true."

"Oh, what's that?" Maxwell's curiosity surprised him. His dad would never have put up with him if he'd decided to stick around Gilead to take on a job in service, but Dad loved eating out. Didn't he realize someone had to facilitate his lifestyle? It didn't do to think of oneself as better than someone else just because he had money, and the other person's job was to cater to him.

"I don't even know. I've never had the chance to find out." Eryn brushed her hair aside as though she removed her concerns with it and smiled at him. "It doesn't matter. So, you're living in Chicago?"

"Not anymore. Montana is home now."

She blinked. "Montana? They call it Big Sky Country, but can it really compare to Kansas?"

Maxwell chuckled. "I live in the hills just west of the Continental Divide. The skies are wider in the east. I've driven across the state a few times on my way to and from Chicago, and it lives up to its nickname."

Was that wistfulness on Eryn's face? How did someone go her entire life and not get to experience life outside her birthplace?

Maxwell wouldn't wish divorced parents on anyone, but having two distinctly separate homes had broadened his horizons right there.

ERYN RALSTON STUDIED the man before her. Memories of Maxwell Sullivan from childhood zipped through her mind, and time had only been good to him. He'd always been slight of build. Now his shoulders had broadened, and those were real muscles visible below the sleeves of his T-shirt. What did he do for a living with biceps like that? The Sullivans had money. There'd be no need for him to take on a menial job.

Not like her.

She needed to say something. Do something, anything besides stare at him. "Your family has a chain of hotels, right? Is that where you work?"

Maxwell nodded. "My grandfather is over 80, but he still heads up the company. My dad and my uncle work for him. I guess all the grandsons do, too, though I struck out on my own for a while."

Eryn tried to imagine a business that employed all its family members. It sure wasn't a wheat farm in Kansas like Dad's. He'd been barely hanging in there before the medical bills from Amelia's accident tipped the balance. Not helpful. Eryn blocked the thought. "Oh? What did you do?"

He shook his head with a self-deprecating smile.

Was that a dimple? How had she not ever noticed a dimple on him back when they were kids? Yeah, he'd been Amelia's thing. If Eryn had learned anything in life, it was never to compete with her twin. Amelia would win, and Eryn would lose. The rules had been simple and reinforced often until Eryn had been trained.

She pulled her attention back to Maxwell, who was speaking.

"I didn't go to college, much to my father's dismay. I found I was good at construction when working on renovations on one of the Sullivan hotels, so I struck out on my own. My crew and I flipped a bunch of houses, and then

7

Grandfather bought a guest ranch in Montana and summoned all us boys out there to fix up the place and put it on the map. I've been working there the past eighteen months now."

"That sounds cool. I love watching those house flipper shows."

He laughed. "It's not like that in real life. We don't gut and renovate a three-thousand-square-foot house to move-in-ready in a week. And the pace is different at the ranch, too. Some of my crew members didn't want to leave the Chicago area, but the ones who stuck with me have been a real asset as we rehab cottages and build new ones. And my grandfather has vision. Next year we'll be adding eight treehouses for guests. That will be a fun challenge."

Eryn tried to imagine the beauty and the delights of that sort of life. Failed utterly. Seeing it would be like Dorothy transported to the wonders of Oz, but that was only a fairy tale. Dorothy might have said there was no place like home — meaning Kansas — but Eryn wasn't sure she'd feel the same if she could escape.

"Someday I'd like to see a place like that. It sounds… delightful."

Maxwell studied her for a moment. "I like Montana a whole lot more than I thought I would. You should come out there sometime. Take a vacation."

Eryn forced a laugh. "That's a nice dream. I can't even remember the last vacation I took."

His grin was lopsided. "Then it's high time, don't you think?"

"If only." She needed a change of topic. Stat. A rich guy like Maxwell — oh, yes, she remembered the Sullivan money — could never understand the realities of the life she wallowed in. Every penny she or Dad earned went into trying to keep the farm afloat.

Eryn didn't need Maxwell Sullivan figuring out her secret and feeling sorry for her. Pity was the worst.

She'd had enough of it to last a lifetime by being the twin left behind. Everyone talked about Amelia's bright light being dimmed too soon. Had it been Eryn? No one would even have missed her.

CHAPTER TWO

Maxwell let himself into his mother's house as quietly as he could, but of course, her miniature poodle greeted him at the door with a series of yaps and growls.

"Max, honey? Is that you?"

He sighed. "Yes, Mom. Sorry, I didn't mean to disturb you."

"No trouble. I was waiting up for you." She appeared in the archway to the great room. "You must have had a better time than you expected to have stayed this late."

"It was okay. Interesting."

Mom beamed. Trust her to read more into that comment than Maxwell had meant. "Let me put on a pot of tea, and you can tell me all about the classmates you spoke with."

The calendar seemed to flip back by 15 years. But she was probably lonely living here by herself. Princess didn't count. The least he could do was humor her in the few days he'd be her guest. "Sure. There's not much to tell, though."

He followed her into the kitchen and took a seat at the long island while she bustled around. "Have you ever considered moving to Montana?"

Mom pivoted on her heel to stare at him, dropping a teabag on the granite counter. "No. Never. Why would I?"

"Just wondered. With Tate and Stephanie and the boys settled there, I thought you might like to be near your grandsons."

"Gilead is home."

"What's keeping you here? You work remotely, and Jewel Lake has great internet coverage since they invested in infrastructure a few years ago."

She fluttered a hand. "My sister. My church. My friends. My volunteer work."

"I think you'd love Montana if you gave it a chance."

Mom swished boiling water inside the teapot and dumped it down the drain before refilling it and adding the teabags. "Why? Aren't you planning on returning to Chicago when Walter's project is complete, if it ever is? Because I'm certainly not moving *there*." She always called her ex-father-in-law, who was also her employer, by his first name.

"Not sure. Montana is growing on me. I might go into construction there when Grandfather stops churning out ideas for me to build."

She huffed. "That won't be until he's dead, and he shows little sign of slowing down for all he's 82."

Maxwell chomped back a comment about how Dad and his brother, Theodore, were convinced Grandfather was losing his marbles. Not a chance. The old man saw right through all their maneuvering.

"Anyway, there's plenty going on around Jewel Lake and Missoula. I'm positive I could keep my crew busy if I decided to put down roots."

Mom's lips tightened. "And who knows about Bryce."

Maxwell nodded. No point in going there with Mom. His middle brother shrugged off responsibility like water off a duck's back, doing the bare minimum to keep on the Sullivan payroll. Someday, Bryce was sure to grow up, but he appeared to be resisting that moment for as long as possible.

She gave her head a shake. "So, who did you see at the icebreaker? What are the plans for the rest of the weekend?"

"I ran into Stuart Brandt and some of his buddies. I can't believe he married Joanie, and they have four kids already."

"He turned into such a fine young man." Mom smiled. "The Bible college is lucky to have him in the Fine Arts department."

"Uh, yeah. I suppose." Maxwell might be miles ahead of his brother in meeting the challenges of adulthood, but Stuart Brandt left them both in the dust. Until tonight, Max had thought he was doing decently with his life. He employed half a dozen workers and paid them well. He'd done some traveling and lived the good life. But had he missed out?

He kind of knew he had. He'd been so focused on his business he hadn't noticed Heather as more than a bright mind with an eye for design and numbers — a rare combination, in his experience — before she'd given her notice last spring and returned to her hometown to marry some guy she hadn't even mentioned to Maxwell beforehand. Would he have had a chance with her if he'd been more proactive?

Maybe. But it likely didn't matter. He'd only lost a couple of nights' sleep on the what-ifs. And then life continued.

"Who else did you talk to?" Mom set a teacup in front of him.

"Eryn Ralston for a bit."

"Poor girl." Mom shook her head. "She's had it rough."

"I was shocked to hear of Amelia's death. Did you know?"

"Oh, that was dreadful. Her car skidded on ice in the very same intersection where her mother died years ago."

"You could have told me."

Mom frowned at him. "I didn't realize you knew them."

"The Ralstons hosted all those sleigh rides and corn mazes back in the day. The twins were in my class." Plus, he'd kind of had a thing for Amelia, not that a junior-high crush mattered 15 years later. Mostly, Maxwell had been focused on escaping Gilead at his first opportunity.

"Oh, that's right. I didn't think much about it. Amelia's accident happened right about the time of Wally and Ashley's. A few weeks later, I think."

"I get it." And he did. Losing her firstborn had spun Mom into quite a spiral there for a while. Tate had come home to stay with her and help with Jamie, who'd been barely a year old.

Maxwell couldn't blame her for the oversight, all things

considered. Besides, what would he have done if he'd known? Come home for Amelia's funeral? Sent a sympathy card? Probably nothing.

"Some of the people from church help Keith out here and there. I think he's fallen on hard times since his daughter died." Mom shook her head and took a sip of tea.

"I'm sorry to hear that." Eryn hadn't mentioned anything, but why would she have? Maxwell was practically a stranger, and a person didn't go around dumping financial woes on strangers. Not unless they were reduced to begging on a street corner with a cardboard sign in one hand and a tin cup in the other.

"Who else did you talk to?"

Maxwell thought over the evening. "No one else for more than a minute or two. Heavenly Brew catered coffee and snacks, there were some games, and a band comprised of some of my former classmates performed. And we got the schedule for the rest of the weekend."

He'd sat beside Eryn during the short program, since they'd been chatting when it started. No need to mention that to Mom, since she already heard wedding bells everywhere. Maxwell's cousin Graham's wedding had been last weekend in Montana, and Mom couldn't stop talking about it. Negatively, because it had taken place at the main lodge at Sweet River Ranch and hadn't been a big society affair in an upscale Chicago venue. Positively, because it was impossible to deny how happy Graham and Cadence were together.

And Paisley Teele had been flashing an engagement ring from another of Max's cousins, Weston. They were planning a spring wedding. No wonder Mom had romance in mind, though Maxwell and Bryce had given her zero reason to believe they were moving in that direction anytime soon.

After tonight, Maxwell had weddings on the brain, too. He'd be 30 in a few weeks. Stuart Brandt had a wife and four kids. Maxwell had no prospects at all.

What had he even accomplished so far in his life?

DAD SHOULD NOT BE SITTING at the kitchen table, gloomily nursing a cup of coffee at 10:00 at night. He glanced up as Eryn entered and offered a wan smile. "Hi."

"Are you okay?" She set her crossbody purse on the closet shelf and kicked her sneakers into the bottom.

Dad shifted his gaze. "I think we need to talk."

A sense of foreboding settled in Eryn's gut. "About what?"

"There's no easy way to start this conversation, so I'll get right to it. Larry Groening offered to buy the farm."

Eryn sagged into the wooden chair around the corner from Dad. "But you said no, right? We'll get on top of this." How? No clue.

He shook his head. "I agreed. He's expanding his market garden and can use the acreage. Maybe I can even work for him."

"But you can't—"

Dad looked over at her with a woebegone expression. "I've been holding you back. What girl your age wants to keep house for her old man?"

"Me!"

"Do you really?" He huffed a laugh. "Or do you just feel sorry for me?"

Eryn opened her mouth to protest but snapped it shut before finally finding words. "We're a team. We're all we have left."

"You should be finding yourself some nice young man. Get married. Have a few kids. I could enjoy having young'uns around again."

"There isn't any guy I want to date, let alone marry." Maxwell's kind eyes and fine form drifted in front of her mind's eye, but that was ridiculous. Just because they'd chatted for 20 minutes and found themselves seated next to one other for the program didn't mean they were anything to each other. She banished the thought.

"I just couldn't hold onto the farm anymore, Rynie. The bank refused to let up the pressure, and my heart's not into fighting any longer. It's time to let go."

She'd be willing to bet this sort of thing never happened in the Sullivan family with all their wealth.

Bitterness does not become you, Eryn. They earned their security.

But had they really? Had Maxwell? Or had he simply lucked out being born into a family with money while she'd drawn the short straw for poverty? Which also didn't change anything.

"I'll work more hours and give you more of my paycheck."

Dad shook his head. "You've done enough. All you could, and more than I deserved. Besides, it's final. I met with Larry and Karen at the lawyer's office this afternoon and signed papers."

"And you're only telling me when it's a done deal?" She surged to her feet and stared down at her father.

"Because I knew you'd fight me, but there was no other way. Believe me, Rynie. I've tried."

"But...

"You're so much like your mother."

"I think you're confusing me with Amelia. She was the beautiful one who could charm the socks off of anyone."

Dad shook his head with a sad laugh. "She might have looked more like your mother, but you have Kendra's spunk and loyalty. Your sister did not have those qualities."

Hard to argue there. Amelia assumed the world owed her a living. She'd flitted through half a dozen different jobs in the years Eryn had worked her way up at Debby's Diner.

"Larry and I haven't confirmed when we need to be out of the house. He'll do the best he can by us, I know that. He's a solid Christian man, a good neighbor."

"Can we rent the house from him?"

"It's no great shakes, Rynie. He might use it for migrant workers for a while, or just tear it down. There's been no money to keep it up." He shook his head and twisted the coffee cup on the table. "I've failed everyone, and you're the only one left to see it."

Eryn rested her hands on his shoulders, only to feel him trembling with pent-up grief. "Dad. You did the best you could. I should have helped more."

"No, Eryn. It's not on the children to bail out their parents. You should look at getting your own place in town in the next few weeks. Start dating. Don't waste your life looking after your old man."

Maxwell's descriptions of western Montana wafted through Eryn's mind. If a person had to start anew, why not a change of scenery? Dorothy might have thought there was no place like Kansas after she'd been in Oz for a while, but personally, Eryn was pretty sure she'd be happy to live someplace else. Anywhere else.

Dad would never move away. And even though he was pushing her out of the nest, she couldn't leave him behind in Gilead.

"After your reunion events, I guess we'll need to face Amelia's bedroom. I wish I were strong enough to do it alone, but I'm not."

Eryn let out a long, shuddering breath. Neither of them had been inside since Amelia's death, unless Dad had snuck in there when Eryn wasn't looking. Doubtful.

"Okay. We can do that." Did she want to? Not even a tiny bit. Time hadn't dulled the dread of going through Amelia's things. Eryn had burned her own high-school journals after her twin's passing. No way did she want anyone to read through those if she died an untimely death. Would she read Amelia's? She'd try not to, out of respect for the dead, but the pull might be too strong.

She squeezed Dad's shoulders once before resuming her seat. "I'll find some boxes. We can start Sunday afternoon. Or I could skip the rest of the reunion. It's not like anyone would notice if I weren't there."

Even Maxwell Sullivan. But it was sweet of him to cross the gymnasium to convey his condolences and chat for a while as though Eryn hadn't been the class wallflower.

"No, no. Enjoy your friends."

As if they were her friends. They'd been Amelia's, for the most part. "It's no problem to skip."

"What's on tomorrow's agenda?"

"Horseback riding at Walker Ridge Ranch in the morning. A round of golf in the afternoon. I can definitely miss that. I haven't golfed in my life, and it's not like I ever will again. And then a catered dinner in the school gym."

"You've already paid to attend everything. Enjoy. Because Amelia's room won't be nearly as much fun."

He made it sound like the reunion events were going to be a laugh a minute. In comparison, maybe he wasn't far wrong.

If Maxwell Sullivan looked her way another time or two, Dad might even be right.

Not that guys like him ever settled down with girls like her.

CHAPTER THREE

W ho here has done any riding?" The owner of Walker Ridge Ranch surveyed the group.

Maxwell stuck up his hand and glanced around him. A bit over half of his former classmates owned up to at least a little familiarity. Not Eryn, though.

"Okay, those with some experience, please pair up with someone who hasn't, and we'll get through this next part more quickly. The horses are saddled up, as you can see. They're all used to greenhorns, so don't worry about that. No one's getting bucked off today. You need to get out to Colorado or Wyoming if you're looking to ride a bronc."

Or Montana or Texas. Not that Maxwell would correct the rancher out loud, because he wasn't completely wrong.

Around him, his former classmates started pairing off with friends, but Eryn stood alone along the edge, looking down at her tennis shoes.

In a few strides, he was at her side. "Hey, want to ride with me?"

She looked up, her blue eyes wide. "Are you sure?"

"Why not?" He shrugged and grinned at her. "Just following directions."

Was that a hint of dismay on her face? "I've never ridden. I probably shouldn't be here today, either. I—"

He touched her arm as she pivoted away. "But you *are* here, so enjoy it?"

"I don't want to be a bother."

"You're not. More than a third of our class doesn't ride, by the looks of it. You're far from the only one."

"I suppose." She bit her lip.

Pairs lined up to enter the corral where a long row of saddled horses stood, reins looped to the posts. Everyone was chatting and laughing as they awaited their turn. Several helpers kept the line moving.

"Come on. Promise I won't bite."

"Sorry. I'm being silly about this. It's just I'm not very athletic."

"You don't need to be." Maxwell grinned at her. "The horse does most of the work. I should warn you, though, you'll feel muscles tomorrow you didn't know you had."

Eryn wrinkled her nose.

She was kind of cute when she relaxed a little. Not that he could fault her for being reticent. She'd never been the outgoing twin, at least, not that he remembered. But it must still seem strange to do things solo when she'd always had Amelia in her life until just two years ago. They'd probably been very close.

Maxwell rested his hand on the small of Eryn's back to guide her to the end of the line. She was a nice height — not too tall and not too short — and where had that thought come from? They were going horseback riding for an hour or two, and after the banquet tonight, he'd probably never see her again.

Eryn flashed him a smile over her shoulder as she stopped behind the Brandts and the Reeders.

Still, would it be so terrible to keep in touch?

Yes, it would. He lived in Montana, and she'd barely left Gilead in her entire life, if she hadn't been misleading him last night. Why would she have fibbed? To make him feel sorry for her? Nah, she wouldn't do that. It must be true.

Either she didn't want to travel, or she hadn't had the opportunity. Which was it? Maxwell glanced at her profile as she looked out over the gently rolling landscape. A winding strip of green revealed where the river ran through Gilead and beyond. A few small ponds and dugouts dotted the farmland.

Where was the Ralston farm again? Over there, next to the Bed of Greens Truck Farm, which was a new addition since he'd been a kid. It looked like a going concern from this vantage point.

"Hey, our turn." He touched her back again.

She seemed startled as she moved forward.

"Hi, Mr. Walker. I'm Maxwell Sullivan, and this is Eryn Ralston. I've done quite a bit of riding, but Eryn hasn't. What have you got for us?"

"Sullivan, eh?" The man nodded. "Heard your old man bought a ranch out west."

"My grandfather, yes."

"You can ride Trigger there. The big black. And you, Eryn, how about Lady? She's the gray mare."

"Okay." She gave a shuddering breath.

"How's your dad doing, Eryn? I haven't had a chance to touch base with him lately."

"Fine."

"Good man, your father."

"I'll tell him you asked about him."

Maxwell shook his head. This was an odd little town where everyone was in each other's business. He could only be thankful he'd escaped all those years ago. "Trigger looks fine, thanks." He turned to Eryn. "Let me help you with Lady, first. Come meet her."

He took Eryn's hand and tugged her over to the mare. Then he leaned in and whispered. "Don't tell Mr. Walker, but I came prepared. Here, give Lady this carrot, and she'll be your friend for life."

She pulled her hand out of his but accepted the carrot. "Just hold it out to her?"

"On a flat palm."

"Ooh!" Eryn giggled as Lady nipped the treat in one bite. "That tickled."

He'd been about to warn her. "Okay, come stand here on Lady's left. Tuck your left foot into the stirrup and grab the saddle horn. Got it? Now give yourself a good boost and swing your right leg over her back."

It took Eryn a couple of tries before she made it into the saddle. "Wow. This is higher than I thought."

"Sit right there." Maxwell turned to Trigger and mounted up, nodding to the rancher. "Hold the reins loosely. I'm guessing she'll follow Trigger no problem."

"That's right, son," the older man agreed. "Looks like you've got it from here."

Maxwell grinned at Eryn before he squeezed his knees gently against Trigger's flanks. "Let's see how this goes."

Was this how his cousin Weston felt all the time when teaching greenhorns to ride at Sweet River Ranch? Because it was gratifying to see the faith Eryn placed in both him and Lady, even though she was obviously terrified... at least, judging by her clenched eyes and white knuckles.

Lady ambled behind Trigger, and Maxwell turned in his saddle slightly. "You're doing great. Enjoy the view. Everything looks better from this vantage point."

Even Kansas.

Even Eryn Ralston.

MAYBE SHE WASN'T GOING to fall off the swaying horse and make a fool of herself in front of everyone. More to the point, in front of Maxwell, who'd been nothing but kind to her since last night.

Men like him never paid attention to women like her, so she should soak it up while she had it. He'd probably jet away from Kansas tomorrow, and she'd never see him again. Just as well, because he made her want things that weren't her lot in life: marriage and a family, sure, but also ease and adventure. No, the greatest role she might be destined for was *cooking* at Debby's Diner, not just assisting.

Big whoop. It might be someone's dream, but not hers.

It was the end of September, and the days were still quite pleasant. She relaxed a tiny bit at the warmth of the sun on her skin and the flicker of breeze playing with her hair. She should have tied it back.

She still couldn't believe she was horseback riding with Maxwell Sullivan. Right, and a whole bunch of other people, but whatever. He was focused on her even now, glancing at her with a smile as she rode behind him. He took his responsibility seriously.

"So, um, tell me about Montana. About the ranch. Is it like Walker Ridge?"

He shook his head. "Not much the same, no. There are quite a few ranches in our area, most of them working spreads."

"What do you mean?"

"Oh, that they earn their income from raising beef cattle and selling them. Sweet River used to be a working ranch, but the folks who owned it maybe ten years ago began turning it into a guest ranch. Some people call them dude ranches."

"So, your ranch's income comes from tourists."

"My grandfather's ranch, but yes. We do have some cows and a small team who cut and bale the hay for the livestock, but our revenue is mostly tourist driven. There's an RV campground, cottages to rent by the week, and hotel rooms in the lodge itself."

"Sounds nice." Eryn tried to come up with a picture in her mind.

"The Sweet River flows through a small lake where our guests swim and paddle and fish. My cousin Weston is the head wrangler, offering riding lessons and trail rides, and his girlfriend is the activities coordinator, coming up with everything from events for kids whose families vacation there to festivities for the Fourth of July."

Every word out of his mouth gave Eryn's imagination one more block to build with as the idyllic picture blossomed. The image was green... greener than anything Gilead offered at any time of year. "How about winter?"

"We can get a boatload of snow overnight, but it's not too bad. The wind doesn't have a chance to roll through the ranch like it does here. We don't have many guests in the winter, just a few at the lodge from time to time, so it's pretty cozy. Fires in the stone fireplace, chess games, good food — my aunt Nadine is the chef, and she keeps us well fed."

Why hadn't Eryn ever thought of other places that hired cooks? Not just restaurants. Huh. Not that she could aspire to being more than a sous chef, but that could be a steppingstone to other options. Not at Debby's, though. She'd never advance there.

If she could do anything, be anything she wanted, would she choose to cook?

Mind-blowing question, and one she had no answer to. And here she was, wasting a brand-new experience on mulling her sad life. Not only riding, but in the company of the sweetest man she'd ever met. Granted, she didn't know him all that well, but wouldn't it be hard to fake the kindness in his eyes? Why would he pretend?

"Thanks again for not making fun of 'fraidy-cat me."

He grinned at her, the skin around his eyes crinkling. "Why would I? Every experience is new to everyone once."

"I bet you've been riding since you were a kid." Although he'd grown up in Gilead, so maybe not.

"I rode a few times at summer camp." He shrugged. "But that was eons ago. Most of my experience has been in the past couple of summers since living at Sweet River. I never had the opportunity in between — didn't look for it, either, to be honest. I was too focused on my business to consider the value of leisure time or the beauty of nature."

"Life gets busy." They could agree on that, at least.

Maxwell studied her. "What do you enjoy for hobbies?"

"Hobbies?" Her gaze flew to meet his. "Does quilting count?"

"Quilts? Definitely. It must take a long time to sew one."

And they were pricy to make, so she couldn't indulge often. A couple of times the fabric store in town had received a custom request and hired her. Those had been tons of fun. "They do take a long time. I've been saving up for a quilting machine. I tried doing one by hand like in the olden days, but it took forever."

"Didn't pioneer women do that in groups? Loads of gossip and tea while they stitched?"

What? How did he know about that?

He chuckled at the expression on her face. "Hey, I read, and I enjoy history. Plus, I came across a stack of cool quilts tucked away in an attic of this one house I renovated, so I had to do some research to figure out if we had true antiques on our hands."

"Did you?"

"No, they weren't that old, so no collectors lined up to buy them. I sold them as a lot but kept one because I liked it."

He'd kept a quilt. What kind of guy was Maxwell Sullivan? He was more nuanced than she'd ever have given him credit for. "I'd love to see it sometime." Whoa. That had been awfully forward of her.

"You'll have to come to Montana, then. Much as I like the quilt, I don't travel with it. I leave it folded on the foot of my bed and have done for several years now. I guess that's how I know where home is."

The only home Eryn had ever known was about to be ripped away from her. Could she choose to see that as a stepping-stone? A blessing? "Maybe I'll take you up on that sometime. I've never traveled, but Montana — your ranch — sounds beautiful." She was lousy at flirting, but it didn't matter. Maxwell would be leaving soon, and she'd be staying.

"It's a great place." He studied her for a minute then swept his hand toward the vista. "This has its own beauty, though."

The other riders had disappeared from view over the crest of a low hill. The landscape was mottled yellow and green, and a neighboring farm settled into a hollow up ahead. To the right, Gilead lay nestled against the winding river.

"Yes, there's beauty here." But it was a harsh beauty, or maybe her view was tainted by the realities of Dad selling out the farm that had been in their family for generations. Her ancestors had managed to hang onto it through two world wars and the Great Depression, but all it took to reverse fortunes these days was a hefty medical bill. If the sacrifice had restored Amelia's broken body to health, it might have been worth it, but it had been too little, too late.

Was she a terrible sister to wish Dad had simply

accepted Amelia's inevitable passing back then the way he seemed to be accepting the loss of the farm now?

On the other hand, Eryn was still here, hale and healthy, and she had an opportunity to look past the Kansas horizon, wide as it might be.

Except she couldn't leave Dad behind.

CHAPTER FOUR

The class reunion had been far more fun than Maxwell ever anticipated, and that was all because of Eryn Ralston. He'd rarely golfed — much to his father's disgust — so he hadn't been much ahead of Eryn on the course. Stuart and Joanie had hung out with them, and two other couples had joined them for the catered dinner in Gilead High School's gymnasium later on.

Maxwell hadn't been a popular kid, but he hadn't been an outcast, either. He just hadn't cared to fit in nor tried all that hard. Eryn had gone through school in her sister's shadow, but she seemed to come out of her shell a little with Joanie and the other women, one of whom worked at the fabric store, Sew Easy.

As the program came to a close, he was strangely reluctant to say goodbye to her. He'd be in Gilead for a few more days. It wouldn't hurt to hang out a bit longer, would it?

Even as he thought it, he knew it *could* hurt. Why

pretend there could be anything between them? He had zero intention of moving back to Gilead. Eryn might sound wistful about traveling in general and seeing Montana in particular, but she was rooted in Kansas by a widowed father and a family farm.

Wasn't it just his luck? The first woman to catch his eye in forever, and there was no future to be had. Not that he knew her well enough to assume a future was a remote possibility.

The program tonight had included a short skit by several class members who worked in the Bible college's drama department, a comedy sketch by a woman who was in national demand as a speaker, and several numbers by the band.

The principal emeritus made his closing remarks and invited everyone to donate to the school's marching band program, which was in dire need of new uniforms and instruments. Maxwell would drop a check off on Monday. Why not? He had no bones to pick with Gilead High. The kids here deserved the best.

Eryn deserved the best, too, but it seemed like her life had been a series of getting whopped by the short end of the stick. Maybe Maxwell's donation could help a few kids from the upcoming generation find hope in a brighter future… like Eryn needed.

The classmates rose and applauded as Mr. Stone left the stage. Maxwell joined them. Beside him, so did Eryn.

She looked lovely tonight in a simple black dress that accented her curves. Her long blond hair flowed with gentle curls. She glanced at him as she clapped, and their gazes tangled for a long moment as something passed between them.

What was it? Maxwell didn't know, but he was going to find out. Maybe geography could be overcome. He'd spent his entire adult life facing puzzles and solving them with aplomb. This was just another brainteaser. He was worthy of the chance to solve it.

Maybe Eryn was, too.

WHAT HAD ALL that been about? For a solid couple of minutes, Eryn found herself unable to break away from Maxwell's gaze. He had stunning brown eyes, deep and unfathomable, a place she could get lost.

Which was all kinds of silly. Eryn didn't do lost, not like that. She'd figured out at a young age that she needed to watch her own back. No one else was going to, especially not her twin. She'd tried to watch Amelia's but had been elbowed aside.

Some people talked about the twin bond, how they were each other's best friend forever, and all that rot. So not true. Not for Eryn. Amelia had always seemed annoyed if she had to share with her and, if Eryn had something she wanted, Amelia simply helped herself.

Now Eryn had Dad all to herself, but that came with a dumpster-sized bucket of guilt. She'd failed him. Failed everyone. Whatever Maxwell was trying to say with that lingering look didn't matter, because if she let herself hope, he'd be her victim, too. Eryn failed herself. No one in her sphere was safe.

Maxwell's shoulder brushed hers as they retook their seats. "You okay? You seem lost in thought."

"I'm fine." She looked away. "It's been a nice evening — a nice weekend. Reality returns in the morning with church." Maybe if she mentioned the church word he'd back off.

"Do you attend Fount of Grace?"

She blinked. "Yes."

"Oh, good. I'll see you again then." He smiled. "That's where my mother goes, as well."

Eryn knew who Maribel Sullivan was, an elegant 50-something woman who sat by herself in the same pew every week and talked to only a few who seemed to be in her social class. It wasn't like Eryn had ever rubbed shoulders with the woman.

Another reminder of how very different her family was compared to Maxwell's. About the only thing they had in common was being in the same grade and having lost a sibling.

And, apparently, church. Did he attend to placate his mother, or did he have a faith of his own? His brother Tate had taken part in the passion play, so at least one of the younger generations believed. Maybe Maxwell did, too.

Did that make any difference to her? Yes, but only for his sake. Their lives still didn't overlap by much. Not by enough.

She'd treasure this weekend for the rest of her life, though. His sweet compassion last night. His delight in talking about Montana and his work at the ranch there while they rode horses at Walker Ridge. His bemused acceptance of how badly he golfed, and his whoop when she'd made that one great swing that sent her ball most of the way down the center of the fairway. A fluke, for sure, but he'd cheered it with her.

And now tonight, he'd been attentively at her side as though it were a real date he'd asked her on, and not simply the culmination of their reunion weekend.

"Would you like to go for coffee after the banquet?"

Eryn blinked at Maxwell. "Coffee?"

"I know it's late." He grinned. "But that's what decaf is for. Someplace in town must be open this late."

Eryn grimaced. "Only the diner, and I'd really rather not go there." She could just imagine all the questions she'd be faced with by her coworkers if anyone caught sight of her with Maxwell outside of the reunion activities. As it was, some of their former classmates already eyed them speculatively. Joanie probably didn't think Eryn was good enough for Maxwell, and she'd be correct. Didn't stop Eryn from enjoying every minute, because it would soon be over.

"I can see that." Maxwell looked thoughtful. "And then there's my mother, who insists on staying up to see me safely home as though I were 18 not 28. Whose parent does that?"

Eryn raised her hand a little and chuckled. "My dad, too." Her grin faded quickly as she recalled the bomb he'd dropped last night after waiting for her.

"You live with him?"

"Yes." Like a loser. She didn't need to see the pity or condescension on Maxwell's face.

"Cool. I bet that works out well for you both."

Eryn blinked. "Um, yes. So far, it has." She didn't need

to dump the sordid details of their current situation on this guy. Maxwell had been nothing but a pleasant diversion this weekend, and who wanted to remember that ending with pity? Not her.

"Is your dad doing okay?"

Did she dare answer honestly? Maxwell would probably think she was begging for money, and she would never do that. Besides, Dad said the farm sale to the Groenings was final. Even Maxwell's wealth couldn't reverse that.

"I can't imagine how hard it's all been for him, losing his wife and his daughter." Maxwell studied her pensively as he went on. "I'm not sure if that would be worse than losing a mom plus a twin, though."

Maxwell, like everyone, assumed Eryn and Amelia had been a tight unit. That was so far from reality, but Amelia was having the last laugh from beyond the grave. She'd always hated the farm, and Eryn and Dad were losing it on account of her medical bills.

Eryn shook her head to dislodge the thoughts. She didn't want to waste them on Amelia when she had Maxwell to herself for a few more minutes. Even now, their classmates' voices grew louder as men helped women with their wraps and began exiting the auditorium. "I guess it isn't a contest. It's been difficult for both of us." In so many ways.

Maxwell rose and shook hands with Stuart as the Brandts left the table, citing a need to get their babysitter home. Then he sat back down and met her gaze. "I have a question for you."

Her answer would be yes. Which was ridiculous, since she didn't know what the question was. "Oh? What is it?"

"I've really enjoyed reconnecting with you this weekend, and I'd like to keep in touch. Would you be open to that?"

She stared at him. What, exactly, did he mean? Because he was leaving, and she was staying. He couldn't possibly mean... no, of course not. There was no way he could possibly be thinking of a long-distance relationship, and no one did pen pals anymore. Were there any other ways to take his question? She couldn't think of any.

Eryn forced a quick smile. "I'm not sure what the point of that would be. I mean, it's been nice seeing you again, too, but..."

Maxwell's pensive smile faded. "Friendship is never wasted, but you're probably right. There'd be no point."

Friendship was noble, and one could never have too many friends. Eryn should know, because she had very few. But friendship with a guy — a handsome, attentive, muscular, wealthy guy — would only make her want all the things she couldn't have.

The thought was so depressing it was all she could do not to burst into tears then and there. She bit her lip and enforced control. "I really appreciate the offer." More than he could ever know. "But I don't see our paths crossing again. At least not until the 20-year reunion."

His dimple showed when he grinned. "I don't want to contemplate being 38. I feel old enough here at the 10-year, except that some people have a busload of kids already. Maybe I've missed the point of life."

Join the party, buddy.

But she wouldn't say that. It was just hard to imagine a man like Maxwell having regrets. Eryn felt the same way whenever she saw Joanie Brandt and her kids around town. Stuart hadn't seemed like a great catch as a teen, but it appeared he was a devoted husband, father, and employee.

Eryn tried for levity. "Are kids the point of life? If so, I guess I've missed it, too."

"I'm sure there's more." His warm brown gaze held hers. "I hate that you turned me down."

She hated it, too. She took a deep breath. "I'm not sure what the end game would be. Friendship is nice, but how would that even work, as far apart as Kansas and Montana are? It's best not to—" She cut off the word 'hope.' He didn't need to know what he'd stirred up in her in only a day.

"It could lead to more. I can't promise that, of course. We barely know each other."

And once he did know her better? He'd back off anyway.

Eryn shook her head. "If life were different…"

The overhead lights flicked off then on a couple of times.

Maxwell looked toward the doors. "I think we're the last ones here, and that was a signal to get moving."

"Probably." Before Eryn could stand, Maxwell was behind her, pulling out her chair. He'd been so attentive and polite and kind all weekend. Maybe she shouldn't be so quick to reject his overture.

Yes, she should. The longer she let herself dream, the more painful it would be when the crash came. And it would come. Guys like Maxwell Sullivan didn't fall for girls like Eryn Ralston.

End of story.

Fairy tales were only fables, after all. They didn't happen to real people. They'd only been written so women like her could escape their sordid realities for a little while and dream of charming princes sweeping them off their feet.

Like Cinderella at the ball, Eryn had enjoyed a couple of amazing days, but her pumpkin of a beater car hadn't turned into a jeweled coach, and Maxwell wouldn't be showing up at her doorstep to see if the glass slipper she'd left behind at the stroke of midnight would fit on her size-eight foot.

It wasn't anywhere near midnight, and she had no glass slippers, just a pair of slingbacks she'd splurged on with her first paycheck when she started busing tables at the diner a decade ago.

Her life would be back to humdrum tomorrow. Or at least after she and Dad had sorted Amelia's belongings.

Ugh.

Getting away had never sounded so good.

CHAPTER FIVE

M r. Ralston? It seems our children have rekindled their childhood friendship the past few days. Would you and Eryn like to come for lunch?"

Maxwell stifled a groan. Why had he ever mentioned Eryn's name more than once in recounting the reunion activities to his mother? She was jumping to conclusions in her desperation to lure Maxwell into staying in Kansas... and she didn't even know he'd briefly nursed the idea until Eryn shot him down last night.

Of course, Eryn was right to have done so, but he still couldn't be impolite to her father. He reached to shake Keith Ralston's hand. "I'm pleased to meet you again, sir. I fondly remember the events out at your farm when we were kids."

The man's face brightened. "Those were the days."

Oh, man. Maxwell had put his foot in it again. The sleigh rides had ended abruptly when Mrs. Ralston had passed away. Best to keep going. "I understand you've also lost your other daughter recently. Please accept my mother's and my condolences."

Mom shot him a sideways glance, but politeness won. It always would. "Yes, Mr. Ralston. I was saddened to hear of it."

Keith bowed his head. "I appreciate that, and I know you've seen your share of grief with your son's passing. Eryn tells me young Jamie has been adopted by his uncle and aunt?"

Eryn's panicked expression toward her father would almost be humorous if the conversation were less painful. Still, she'd talked to her dad about their conversations. Was that good or bad?

It doesn't matter. She doesn't want a long-distance friendship.

Not that he'd been angling for merely friendship, but they'd only just reconnected. It was far too early to say he wanted to see if they could be more.

Mom's lips pursed. "Yes, Tate and Stephanie live in Montana with Jamie and their baby boy, Simon."

"Long ways away, Montana."

"Very." Mom skewered Maxwell with a look.

What, as though he were going to stay in Gilead because she didn't want to uproot and move to Jewel Lake? Not happening.

"But that's neither here nor there," Mom segued smoothly. "What do you say to lunch? Dominica — my cook — has prepared a repast too much for just Maxwell and me."

At Mom's request, no doubt. It's not like Dominica acted on her own.

Eryn closed her eyes briefly before turning to Mom with a wan smile. "Thank you, Mrs. Sullivan. That's lovely of you, but Dad and I have a full day planned. Maybe some other time."

She meant when Maxwell wasn't home. That kinda hurt.

Keith glanced between them, obviously confused. "Well, we need to eat, one way or the other, so what could it hurt? I say yes, we should go."

"Excellent." Mom nearly purred. "We're at 110 Killion Place. You can follow us home or come on your own. And Eryn?"

"Yes, ma'am?"

"That's Maribel to you, not Mrs. Sullivan. Maxwell's father and I have been divorced for many years, and the title of missus no longer suits."

"Yes'm. I mean, Maribel. Thank you." Eryn shot a glance at Maxwell.

He had nothing for her. Mom had been a stickler in that regard since she'd kicked workaholic Dad out 15 years back. Dad had cheerfully moved to Chicago, where he'd practically lived, anyway. With no distractions of wife and kids, he'd poured all his energy into Sullivan Enterprises as Grandfather's right-hand man. When each of his boys graduated from high school, he'd welcomed them into the family business as adults.

Win, win for Dad. Not so much for Mom.

"See you in a few minutes." Mom nodded to Keith and Eryn as she tucked her hand in the crook of Maxwell's elbow. She acknowledged a few other parishioners with a smile and shook hands with the pastor as they exited the building.

Maxwell opened the car door for his mother then leaned in after her. "What are you trying to prove with that invitation?"

"You seem to need a little help."

"I do not need help. You may have forgotten I live at Sweet River Ranch, and—"

"Temporarily." She waved a hand. "Walter will run out of projects one of these days, and—"

"And then, like I already told you, I'll make my home in Jewel Lake and hang out my shingle as a contractor. I'll build houses and take on renovations."

"Which you could do right here in Gilead."

"Mom, I'm not moving back."

"Not even for the right girl?"

He shook his head as he held her gaze. "This is not my home anymore."

"But it could be again."

Wow, she was stubborn. Maxwell might have gotten his workaholic tendencies from his father, but his doggedness? All from Mom. No wonder he'd left town the day after graduation. He and his mother had butted heads over nearly everything the last couple of years when he was the only remaining kid in the nest.

"I don't know how to make this any more plain, but your plan isn't going to work. I'm not rude enough to go over to Keith Ralston and tell him not to come for lunch, but you need to stop trying to manipulate me. Got it?"

Mom pursed her lips and shot daggers with her eyes. "Be careful how you talk to your mother."

He closed the car door and rounded the vehicle. Across the parking lot, Keith and Erin clambered into an older gray truck. Maxwell lifted his hand in acknowledgment, but he was distracted. How was he going to get through to his mother?

Maybe he wasn't. Maybe he'd have to put up with her machinations for two more days before she drove him to the Wichita airport. Eventually, she'd forget her idea when nothing happened between him and Eryn.

Besides, Mom wasn't thinking straight. At the moment, she was desperate for Maxwell to meet someone. Anyone. But long term she was also too snooty to think a Ralston was good enough for a Sullivan.

He slid into the driver's seat of her electric car, pressed the starter button, and shifted into gear. There wasn't anything more to say, so he didn't bother trying. Best just to let her figure it out for herself.

"Why did you take Maxwell's business card?" Eryn had barely been able to hold the question until they were in the truck on the way back to the farm. "You sold the farm, so you don't need any renovations done." And the thought was still bitter.

"Why not? He seems a nice young man, and he likes you." Dad winked. "You could do worse."

She glared at him. "Don't fall in with his mother. It doesn't become you." And why did Maribel seem to be so eager to get to know Eryn? Didn't the woman realize how far beneath the Sullivans the Ralstons were?

"Aw, Rynie. I want you to be happy. And rich would be okay, too."

"Dad!"

"Just stating the facts in privacy here."

"Don't get any ideas."

"Did you not notice how that boy kept looking at you?"

Eryn's skin itched. "He didn't. This is all something you've conjured up in your head."

"He hung out with you during every event this weekend. He wouldn't have done that if he didn't like you. I don't know why I need to remind you men know how to avoid women they can't stand. They don't seek them out."

Eryn stared out the truck window. "He was just being nice. Everyone else had friends there."

"And why don't you?" Dad's voice gentled. "Have friends, I mean. You're so focused on your job that you don't get out much. I hadn't realized you didn't get out *at all.*"

Tears pricked Eryn's eyes. "They were all Amelia's friends, not mine. She was the popular one."

"She was like a butterfly, that's true. But she would have been happy to include you."

Eryn pivoted to look at her father. "Who wants to be a pity project? Not me. And besides, she didn't want—" Oh, no. She'd never meant to air her problems with Amelia to him. Let him remember his other daughter — his favorite one — the way he'd seen her.

Dad's brow furrowed as he studied her.

"The road, Dad."

"I'm paying attention."

Did he mean to the road... or to her? Eryn didn't even want to know. "Look, don't worry about it, okay? It doesn't matter anymore."

"It seems it matters to you."

"Nope. I'm all good. That was a rare moment." *Liar, liar, pants on fire.*

"Are you sure you're up for clearing out her bedroom this afternoon? Because we can do it another time."

Eryn took a sharp breath and then exhaled. "Today is good. I brought home boxes from behind the grocery store last night. Because you're in an all-fired hurry to get rid of our home."

"Rynie, that's not how it is."

"It's how it seems. I'll manage. I just don't like change."

"Sometimes change is needed to shake things up a bit."

She gritted her teeth. Dad needed things shook up? Fine. He didn't need to drag her along with him.

They'd finally arrived at the farmhouse. Eryn jumped out, popped the trunk on her car, and grabbed an armload of collapsed boxes. "I'm heading in there right now."

"I thought we might have a cup of tea first."

"You had tea at the Sullivans'. Don't wimp out on me, Dad. You started this, and you're coming in with me from the first minute."

He took a shuddering breath. "Okay, okay. But I don't even know where to start."

"How about you start by stripping the linens and throwing everything in the wash? Then you can dismantle the frame. It will give us room to stack boxes."

"What will we do with the bed?"

47

"The college thrift store can pick it up when we're ready." Like her dad, Eryn had been putting off this job, but now that they'd agreed, she was ready to purge the remains of Amelia's life. Maybe that would help with the ugly memories. Maybe a fresh start in a home her sister had never lived in would help, too.

She could only hope so as she stood in the doorway. The room was a mess — a mess with a solid layer of dust over everything.

Eryn crossed the space, opened the window, and looked back at her dad. Tears had filled his eyes, and his chin was quivering. She strengthened her resolve. "I'll go through her clothes."

"If you see anything you'd like, keep it. You were about the same size."

"I'll keep that in mind." No, she wouldn't. A purge was a purge.

Eryn did her best to ignore her father as he cleared the bed and banged it apart with a hammer. She stood at the closet and folded item after item into boxes for the thrift shop, except for the ones stuffed in the back that showed too much wear. Those went into a trash bag. She could use some of the empty hangers, but the rest got boxed.

There, that had been therapeutic. Next came the litter of shoes mounded on the closet floor. There were a few cute pairs that Eryn might've been tempted to snag if Amelia's feet hadn't been a size smaller.

Now on to the dresser. Most of the contents were trash. No one wanted used underwear. In the bottom drawer, beneath Amelia's summer nighties, lay a pile of journals.

Eryn glanced up to see Dad disappear through the doorway lugging the headboard.

She'd just tuck those books in her own room and burn them later. Would that be before or after she'd read some of them?

Dad was downstairs.

She'd take a quick peek before getting back to sorting. The covers had the years neatly penned in Amelia's round handwriting. The last one was the year she'd died. Eryn wasn't sure if she wanted to know what Amelia thought of life that recently. More than a dozen years' worth of memories. Maybe she could handle reading about junior high.

The first journal was from seventh grade, the year before Mom died. Eryn bent the paper cover and let the pages flick by in a buzz. She shouldn't read these private thoughts. But maybe she'd understand Amelia a bit better if she did. Maybe there'd be some sort of closure if an entry mentioned a desire to be closer to her twin.

It was a long shot, but it wasn't completely impossible.

January 1, 2008

We had our annual sleigh ride this afternoon for kids from school. There was barely enough snow, but it was still fun. Then Mom made hot chocolate and cookies. Yum. But what's really yummy is Max. Sigh. He's so cute with his dark curly hair!!! [three heart emojis] I think maybe he likes me!!! [three heart emojis]

Eryn slapped the book closed. She did *not* want to read about her sister's adolescent crush on Maxwell Sullivan.

On the other hand, maybe she'd get some insight on what made the man tick. Not that any of it mattered.

Amelia was dead, and Maxwell was leaving for Montana again on Wednesday.

It couldn't possibly hurt to indulge in a little nostalgia, even if it was through her sister's eyes. Could it?

"Eryn?"

"Coming, Dad. I just took a little break, but I'm ready to get back at it."

CHAPTER SIX

Maxwell had told himself a dozen times since yesterday that this was a bad idea. He should leave well enough alone.

But still, he'd called Debby's Diner to find out if Eryn were working, and the helpful waitress said not until 4:00. Given she didn't seem to be a social butterfly, that meant she was likely at home.

She'd been clear about not wanting to pursue anything with him. He'd also set his mother straight. No relationship. No friendship, even. Just a couple of days catching up on old times with an acquaintance before moving on.

Which was a bunch of crock, because he didn't have that many memories with Eryn in them. None without her twin. And they hadn't discussed ancient history for more than five minutes of their conversations.

No, she was intriguing, and he couldn't quite put his finger on why. She seemed vulnerable. She seemed like she needed a champion. In fact, Eryn reminded him of several workers on Maxwell's crew who'd just needed a simple leg up so they could blossom and prosper on their own.

Everyone needed someone to believe in them.

Maybe he should offer her a job as he had to Heather, to Jordan, to Janessa.

That was the thought that sent him to the Ralston farm on Monday morning. He hadn't been here since — think, think — the winter before Mrs. Ralston's accident? Even as a kid, he'd been intrigued by buildings and architecture, and now, as he pulled into the farmyard, problems leaped out at him. The porch roof drooped. The siding needed fresh paint and, in some places, repairs. The double-hung windows were the inefficient kind that leaked air.

Frowning, Maxwell parked his mother's car between Keith's truck and Eryn's car then climbed out. The Ralstons had either fallen on hard times or simply neglected their home. A quick glance around caused him to amend his thoughts to include the barn and machine shop. Bringing this place up to par would run an easy couple of hundred grand. Probably more.

Not that anyone had asked for his professional opinion.

Maxwell mounted the steps, careful of where he set his feet, and knocked on the wooden door.

A moment later, the door opened to reveal a surprised Keith Ralston. "Hello. Maxwell. I didn't expect to see you here."

"I came to see Eryn before I leave for Montana. Is she home?"

"Uh, sure. We were just finishing up a project." The man grimaced slightly. "We'd never dealt with Amelia's room, and we're doing that now, along with everything else."

What kind of everything else? "I won't interrupt if you're busy. I came by on a whim."

"No, no. Come on in." Keith widened the opening and beckoned. "We're at a good stopping place."

"Dad? Who was at the door?" Eryn jogged down the stairs just far enough for her gaze to meet Maxwell's. "Um, hi. I wasn't expecting to see you."

Maxwell offered an easy grin. "Surprise! But I don't need to stay. Your dad says you're busy."

"We have time for tea." Keith gave his daughter a pointed look. "I'll go put it on."

Eryn's hand touched her adorably messy ponytail. A bit of dirt smudged her cheek and her old jeans and T-shirt. "I'll be right back." She disappeared upstairs.

Awkward. Maxwell stood in the small entry. The staircase looked solid for the era, but refinishing would bring out its natural beauty. The house also had high ceilings edged with wide moldings. It could look quite charming.

Somehow, he didn't think offering to renovate their home would be taken well. Probably they couldn't afford it, or they'd have done it already, and besides, Maxwell was not moving back to Kansas, remember?

Yeah, he remembered.

Maxwell followed Keith to the kitchen, which would definitely require gutting... He needed to turn that part of his brain off. But why were boxes stacked in the corner and cupboard doors open to reveal empty shelves? He chuckled. "Looks like you guys are moving."

"We are." Keith glanced over from where he set three mugs on the countertop.

Maxwell blinked. "Pardon me?" And why hadn't Eryn mentioned it?

The man sighed and glanced toward the doorway as though checking for his daughter's presence. "We've hit on some hard times, and I sold the farm to Larry Groening the other day. We've got a bit of time, but we tackled Amelia's room yesterday and then sort of kept going. A lot of this stuff has never been used since Kendra passed away." He lifted a shoulder in a shrug that belied the moisture in his eyes.

"Where are you moving?"

"Don't know yet. We'll find a place in town. I can maybe work for Larry — he has that Bed of Greens Truck Farm. Or maybe I can stock shelves at the Co-op. I guess I'll see what crops up. Bad time of year, though."

"But… you're a farmer. You'd hate being cooped up in a feed store or something like that."

Keith grimaced as he shook his head. "You're right, but even without the farm sucking me dry, bills don't pay themselves. Leastways that I've noticed."

A problem a Sullivan grandson had never faced, although Bryce had seemed ready to test the theory at times in his life. He might only be putting in time now, but he was at least earning his keep with landscaping at the ranch.

"I'm really sorry to hear that."

"Dad!"

Maxwell turned to see Eryn with her hands on her hips, glaring at her father. Her hair had been brushed into a high ponytail, and the smudge was off her face. Also, had she dabbed on a little makeup?

He was no expert, but it seemed likely. Maxwell forced himself not to grin at the thought.

"Eryn!" Keith mimicked his daughter's tone and stance. "There's no point in trying to keep it a secret. Everyone in Gilead will know by next weekend, or by tomorrow if Mrs. Alleghany finds out sooner. It is what it is."

Eryn's mouth tightened. "I suppose you're right, but I don't have to like it."

Keith huffed and turned away. "I'm going out to the deep freeze for those cookies Karen sent over the other day."

And off he went, leaving Maxwell with Eryn, whose lips were tight as she glared after her father.

Oh, boy. Maxwell was in the middle of it now. "Hey, it's okay. Nothing to be ashamed of."

She turned her piercing blue eyes on him. "I'm sure you wouldn't know anything about that sort of thing."

"You have me there, but that doesn't mean it's not true."

"Why are you here, Maxwell? Because as soon as your mother knows Dad lost the farm, she definitely won't want us seeing each other. Not that we are. Or want to be."

She was cute when she was flustered, but Maxwell was smart enough not to smile. This was a serious, life-changing moment they'd found themselves in.

And Maxwell was a problem solver, so his mind had instantaneously jumped the tracks in search of solutions.

What had Weston said the other day about Joseph, the guy who ran the farming operations at Sweet River? He was hoping to retire soon. Wasn't that it?

"Excuse me a minute." Maxwell pivoted on his heel as

he pulled his phone out of his pocket and made for the front door.

"Can't get out of here fast enough now?" Eryn mocked.

"I'll be right back for that cup of tea. Cookies also sound good." Maxwell headed to the car for a modicum of privacy and tapped his cousin's number. "Hey, Weston? I've got a question for you."

"WHERE DID HE GO?" Cookie tin in hand, Dad looked around the kitchen.

"Who knows?" Eryn shook her head. "He zipped out of here like the house was on fire, but he said he'd be back."

She doubted it, because why would he? If Maxwell, like his mother, had assumed some sort of prosperity, he'd be off to Montana on the next flight. He'd never bother with a pauper. All of which didn't matter, because that was only the most obvious reason they weren't suited for each other.

Amelia had drooled over the cute boy he'd been more than once in that journal.

Not that Eryn wanted to continue reading… except it was impossible to stop.

"Okay." Dad opened the tin and set some of the cookies on a plate.

Eryn fixed the tea. Three cups because, who knew, Dad might be right.

"Sorry about that." Maxwell reappeared in the doorway. "I had a phone call I needed to make." He looked between Eryn and Dad as though he thought it mattered to them.

She needed to get her head on straight. Dealing with

her twin's things — especially the diaries — had taken its toll on Eryn's optimism. Not that she had much of that naturally. Life had been too hard to cling to it.

None of it was Maxwell's fault. He wasn't part of the problem, and he wasn't part of the solution. She could enjoy another half hour in his presence before saying a permanent farewell. Hadn't she done that yesterday? Yet here they were again.

"The tea is ready. Do you take anything in yours?" She transferred the three cups to the table.

"Honey if you have some, or sugar is fine."

Eryn nodded. "We have honey." She set the little squeeze bear on the table and took the seat nearest the stove.

Maxwell sat around the corner from her, across from Dad, and accepted a peanut butter cookie from the plate. He stirred honey into his tea before looking between them again. "Keith, what kind of equipment does wheat farming require?"

Eryn blinked. Of all the questions she might have dreamed he'd ask, this was not one of them.

"The usual. Tractor, combine." Dad shrugged.

"You use big equipment here? How many acres is this place?"

"Two hundred. I've been farming it for 30-some years and never made enough to buy into the fancy machines. I've got the basics. You in the market for equipment? I can show you."

"No, that's not it." Maxwell looked between them again then leaned forward on the table. "We talked yesterday about the guest ranch my grandfather bought in Montana.

We're dependent on the tourist industry there, but we also have a herd of cattle and the hayfields to sustain them."

Where was he going with this? Eryn tried to keep her face neutral, but Dad looked intrigued. Right. In her experience, men bonded over engines and farms.

"We don't grow grain at all on our spread. We haul that in from further east, but mostly we feed the cows alfalfa hay. The horses like it, too, but of course we supplement with grains as needed."

"We haven't had any horses around here since..." Dad swallowed. "Since we gave up doing the sleigh rides years back."

"My cousin Weston is in charge of our livestock, which includes the farming aspect. He'd said something the other day about the farm manager planning his retirement." Maxwell shot a glance at Eryn too quick to decipher. "I just gave Weston a call to make sure I had my facts straight, and I do. Keith, we have a vacancy for a man of your experience. Sweet River Ranch pays well, and there is staff housing available. Would you consider moving northwest?"

The cookie Dad held halfway to his mouth dropped to the table, bounced once, and landed on the floor. Which demonstrated how Eryn felt, too.

Tears filled Dad's eyes, something that had become far too commonplace since Amelia's death, but there was also a smile. "You mean that, boy? You don't know me or my work ethic. I can't recommend myself, because I can't even make a go of it here."

"I've heard nothing but good about you around town." Maxwell held up both hands. "Not that I've been asking, but people noticed your daughter and I together at the reunion events."

Eryn had an idea which classmates might have tried to either warn Maxwell away from her or encourage him.

"The offer stands. I'm a man of my word."

Dad rubbed both temples as he stared at the table for a long moment.

Eryn held her breath. Something akin to hope rose in her. Was a fresh start, far from Kansas, in the cards for them both? Because surely if Dad took this offer, she'd go, too. Montana! Land of skies even wider than those of Kansas? Home of mountains and plains, lakes and rivers.

"What do you say, Rynie?" Dad looked her way with more anticipation on his face than she'd seen in the past two years.

"I think you should go."

"Me? What about you?" Dad looked at Maxwell then back.

Maxwell turned to her. "We have numerous employment opportunities at Sweet River, Eryn. I'm sure we can find a place for your talents to shine."

"I have no talents."

"Pshaw!" Dad exclaimed. "You have many talents. You've just been hiding them."

She wanted to be angry, but he wasn't wrong.

"What do you say, Eryn?" Maxwell's hopeful eyes smiled at her. "Sweet River will be a better place if you come."

And there went her biggest reason for not accepting Maxwell's offer to keep in touch as friends. Agreeing to a job there seemed like she was saying more, and she wasn't sure she should.

On the other hand, she couldn't let Dad move all that distance by himself and leave her behind. Not if she had a chance to change her life's direction... and maybe find love.

It wouldn't do to look too eager, though.

"We can consider the possibilities."

Dad laughed, the deep lines etching his face lessening a little.

Maxwell threw both hands in the air and did a seated victory dance, his smile big enough to reveal that dimple.

Eryn was so, so in trouble.

CHAPTER SEVEN

So... you're requesting we hire your wannabe girlfriend?" Linking his hands behind his head, Tate leaned back in his office chair. His eyebrows tilted up, accentuating his knowing grin.

Maxwell spread his hands wide. "I cannot affirm or deny. I barely know her, so all this could go south. That's a risk I'm willing to take and, I guess, a risk I'm asking Sweet River Ranch to take on my behalf."

"You do know it's October now, right? Most of our staff is seasonal. Summer, in case you'd forgotten, which is over."

"I'm aware." Why was his big brother making him sweat this out?

"Bro." Tate shifted so he was leaning across his desk. "I have to ask. Is this a knee-jerk reaction to Heather leaving?"

Maxwell skewered his brother with a glare. "Heather quit five months ago. Any jerking of knees is long past.

And, besides, we didn't have that kind of chemistry. We were friends comfortable in each other's company."

"Chemistry?" Tate's voice tilted up with humor. "What kind of chemistry are we talking?"

"Look, I can hire Eryn to my crew if you're going to be like this. I can use an extra person or two, so long as they're willing to learn and follow orders."

Tate chuckled. "Ooh, touchy. But I can see how you'd rather not be her boss if you've got designs on her. What's her skillset? Let's see what we can do." He bumped his mouse and peered at his computer monitor.

Designs. Was that what they were calling it now? It sounded unsavory compared to the growing hope Maxwell felt inside himself when he thought of getting to know Eryn.

Tate's gaze slid to him then back to the screen. "You're taking a big risk, you know."

"Yeah, I know." Maxwell flexed his hands. "But finding out her dad didn't have a job and neither of them had a place to live, I couldn't shut up when I had a solution."

"I think we've heard a rendition of this story before," Tate muttered, jabbing at a few keys.

It took Maxwell a minute before he burst out laughing. "Oh, man. I'd forgotten completely. You offered Stephanie a job as Jamie's nanny when you'd known her for less than a day."

"And then there was Graham, rescuing Cadence after she was jilted, and hauling her all the way from Chicago to give her a job and a fresh start."

Two happily-ever-afters had started in a similar way. Huh. Maybe it wasn't such a long shot, after all.

Tate looked at him again. "I feel obliged to remind you that this is a bigger deal. With Keith Ralston on payroll — great find, by the way; we need him — Eryn may feel obligated to you and like she can't quit her job if things don't work out between you."

"I thought of that." A heavy sigh slipped out of Maxwell. "But I still couldn't leave it be. Keith is a perfect replacement for Joseph. Farming at its core can't be that different in Montana than Kansas. He has all the experience needed to jump straight in."

"We don't have any openings on the resort side, unfortunately. What job experience does Eryn have?"

"Mostly restaurant work. Everything including some cooking."

"Hmm. Aunt Nadine could probably use someone part-time with Emma and Tina away at college. We do have more guests booked over the winter than last year."

"I'm not sure that's what Eryn really wants, but I'm sure she'll be happy with it, at least for now."

Tate studied him, eyes twinkling. "And what does Eryn really want? Besides, assumably, a giant rock on her left hand?"

"She's not a gold digger. If she were, she wouldn't have turned me down when I first asked if we could keep in touch."

The grin widened. "Now there's a story of humiliation I'd like to hear."

"There's nothing to it. She only agreed because her dad decided to accept my offer. She wasn't playing a long game, because she had no way of knowing it was an option. I didn't know when I asked her that, either. I only found out her dad had sold the farm after the fact."

"See, that concerns me. I'm a little reluctant to turn over the farm to someone who lost his own through *hard times*." Tate air-quoted the words. "What does that even mean?"

"You can ask him yourself. Frankly, I didn't think it was any of my business. You'll be his boss, not me."

"I can ask and probably will, but unless he's on the run from the law, you've kind of committed me to hiring him. He's already on his way to Montana."

What day was it? Maxwell had flown home on Wednesday, so it must be Thursday. "They're not leaving Kansas until Monday. Go ahead and set up a video call." He crossed his arms and stared at his brother.

"No, I trust you."

"Good. It didn't sound like it there for a minute." Maxwell let out the breath he hadn't realized he was holding. "Look, I get this is irregular, yours and Graham's experiences notwithstanding. And I also realize I barely know Eryn, and we might not hit it off. But thank you for taking the chance with me."

"Anytime, bro." Tate laughed. "Okay, that's a lie. You get one shot at inviting a wannabe girlfriend to be on staff here. If this is your move, I'll support it."

"I only need one shot."

Tate's eyebrows twitched above his twinkling eyes. "All right. So, I can assign staff housing #4 to them until Joseph moves out of the original farmhouse, probably end of November. The duplex will seem small to them, but that's what there is. At least it has two bedrooms."

Maxwell nodded. He still lived in one of the units over

the winter, when the influx of summer staff flowed back from whence they'd come. In the summer, he lived in his travel trailer surrounded by the campers and tents of his crew. He'd be moving into #9 himself now that he was home. As if the barebones unit could be called home.

Tate had built a house when he'd decided to marry Stephanie and stay in Montana. Graham and Cadence were discussing building sites. Weston had already staked claim to a small plot near the stables for a log cabin for him and Paisley.

Settling on the ranch forever wasn't in Maxwell's plans, not if he opened his own construction company after he'd burned through Grandfather's ever-expanding list of projects. Jewel Lake, though? He could see that. Close enough to be part of things with his family at the ranch, but not involved in the day-to-day.

Eryn might want to have a say in that.

Maxwell blinked. Whoa, his thoughts had totally escaped again. He shouldn't be imagining a future with her like that. Not at this fragile, early point. They mightn't ever even date.

But he was a planner. A forward thinker. That was how he'd more than doubled his nest egg in eight years. He could analyze possibilities, choose a path at the snap of his fingers, and commit to it until completion.

Maybe a woman wouldn't want to be treated like a project that way, but it was who Maxwell was. He couldn't change himself, and why should he? Eryn — he corrected himself — *whomever* he married would think his personality was an asset, not a liability.

Eryn and her dad expected to arrive Wednesday

evening with all their worldly possessions in their two vehicles and a utility trailer hitched to Keith's truck.

Maxwell had a week to prepare. He cracked his knuckles. He was so ready.

"Wow, I can't believe you're all packed up and moving out of Gilead!" Letty, the owner of Heavenly Brew, hugged Eryn Sunday after church.

"I know. It's been a crazy week." Eryn glanced around the foyer of Fount of Grace Fellowship. She'd attended here nearly every single Sunday of her life, other than when she'd been sick. They'd rarely even been on vacation, thanks to the farm.

She was going to miss these people: Pastor George. Zoey and Connor Hamelin. The Groenings.

Joanie Brandt approached. "Wow, girl! Good on you for grabbing that guy so quickly!"

Letty's ears perked up.

"It's not like that. He offered Dad his dream job, and I'm just tagging along."

"You tell yourself what you need to hear."

"Ooh, tell me more!" Letty interjected.

"There's nothing to tell." Eryn wrapped her arms around the middle. "I reconnected with Maxwell Sullivan at the reunion, and when he found out Dad had sold the farm—" a fact Eryn was still getting used to "—with no firm plans, Max offered him a job at his family's ranch in Montana. They have cows and hayfields and all that as well as a guest ranch for tourists. I'm just tagging along."

Joanie and Letty shared a conspiratorial look.

"Whatever you think is going on, that isn't it. I barely know Maxwell. He was always more Amelia's friend than mine when we were kids." A fact that had become clearer as Eryn worked her way through Amelia's journals. She'd given up all pretense of ignoring the temptation with the first mention of Maxwell's name.

"Eryn?"

The two women stepped aside at Maribel's approach.

Maxwell's mother proffered a large container. "I took the liberty of having Dominica prepare some muffins and sandwiches for your trip. I know it's not much, but you and your father may not always have a decent restaurant on hand when you're hungry. The drive between here and Montana goes through desolate terrain." The woman shuddered delicately.

Desolate? Eryn and Dad had poured over online maps to determine their route, and that was not the word she'd have used to describe the scenery. She'd see the Rocky Mountains for the first time and soon be living nestled in their flank! Sign her up.

"Thank you." She accepted the container. "How very thoughtful of you."

Had Letty snickered? Eryn could ignore that.

"I hope you have a good trip, and I'm sure I'll see you when I next visit the ranch."

"Oh?" How hadn't she realized Maribel made the trip? Of course, she would. All her sons lived there plus her two grandsons.

"I work remote for Sullivan Enterprises, and there are semi-annual board meetings. Since Walter bought the ranch, the meetings have been there, but I believe the next one will be back in Chicago. But I also visit for family reasons, when my ex-husband can be bothered to fly me there." Maribel tightened her lips.

Maxwell had mentioned his parents' not-so-amicable divorce.

"I look forward to seeing you next time you come, in that case." Eryn tapped the container. "I can return this then."

"That won't be necessary. It's an extra. I expect to visit for Thanksgiving, even if I have to fly commercial."

A fate worse than death itself, by the sounds of it. Eryn wouldn't know. When she'd told Maxwell she'd rarely been out of Kansas, she meant by car. Planes were beyond her experience.

"I'll see you then." Maribel started to turn away and bumped into Dad. "Oh, excuse me, Keith. I just gave your daughter a bit of food for your trip. I hope it helps."

"That's very kind of you." Dad smiled at the woman before turning to Eryn. "You ready? I thought maybe there was no point in waiting until morning. We can get a few hours' head start today since everything is already packed but our toothbrushes."

Eryn blinked. "Um, sure. You're right. There's no reason to wait." Normally, she'd worry about the extra night in a hotel, but Sullivan Enterprises had issued generous funds for relocation. She'd also received a small bonus with her final paycheck from Debby's.

"What will you be doing at the guest ranch?" Joanie asked.

Letty jabbed her elbow into Joanie's side and they both snickered before glancing at Dad and Maribel and straightening up.

"I'll be kitchen staff. That's my skillset, after all." Eryn had been a bit disheartened with that appointment, but Maxwell had stressed there would be an opportunity to try something else later on, if she wanted. Cooking was fine. People needed to eat. She got that. But she wanted to experience all that Montana beauty, not be cooped up in a stuffy kitchen.

"Sounds fun. I love me a good kitchen and prepping food people will love."

Right, Letty owned a coffee shop. Of course, she'd be a fan.

Why was everyone still watching her? Eryn didn't love being the center of attention like this. "I'm just thankful to have a job waiting for me in the off-season."

"Well, keep in touch, girl." Joanie reached in for a hug and whispered in her ear. "Invite Stuart and me to the wedding."

Eyes wide, Eryn jerked out of Joanie's arms. "There won't—" Best to zip her mouth, since Dad and Maribel were still right here. Talking to each other, but they'd surely overhear any vehement denial.

Joanie winked. "You say that now, but you wait and see. It'll come."

Letty hugged Eryn. "I can guess what Joanie said, and that goes for me, too. Shh." Then she linked arms with Joanie and dragged her away, tossing a wink over her shoulder.

"What was all that about?" Dad asked.

"Nothing much."

But Joanie had voiced the tiny, tentative hope buried deep in Eryn's heart. What did it matter if Amelia had dreamed of the boy Maxwell? She wasn't here to claim the grown man. Could Eryn?

CHAPTER EIGHT

Wednesday.

Maxwell had been patient. Eryn was driving an older car without Bluetooth and, besides, she wasn't dating him. He couldn't expect her to update him on their whereabouts every hour. No, he'd been relegated to a daily text when she and her father stopped for the night. Sometimes she answered his reply, but not always.

Patience. Not a virtue that came naturally.

They'd left Kansas a day early, but instead of pushing through, they'd spent yesterday in Yellowstone and were coming the rest of the way today.

Anytime now.

Not that he was watching the approach to the lodge from his easy chair in the great room. Except, he was. He'd been around long enough to know which seating had a view of the drive, but he wasn't only staring out the window. He had his laptop open while he worked on his computer-assisted-drafting program. CAD had come a long way in the past eight years, and he could make quick adjustments then pivot to see the treehouse design from every angle.

These units on the new Eagles' Nest Lane were going to be epic. At first, they'd planned to keep them dry, but Maxwell's determined research had discovered possibilities for adding plumbing. Of course, that increased both the cost and time involved in each treehouse. They'd build eight over next season and evaluate after a couple of years.

Working? Maybe not so much, since his screen had blanked twice in the past few minutes. How long did it take to drive from Bozeman? Three or four hours? They should be here by now unless one of the vehicles had broken down. Keith would have the use of a staff truck soon enough, but Maxwell couldn't think of any way to upgrade Eryn without her agreement, one he was pretty sure she wouldn't readily give.

Impatience could cost him a chance with her. Not every solution needed to be tied up in a neat bow in as short a time frame as possible.

Over in the kitchen, Aunt Nadine's favorite worship playlist provided background music while she prepped the evening meal for the remaining staff. Sounds of cupboard doors opening and closing, the clank of a pan landing on the stovetop, and the gush of water from the faucet came to his ears.

But then a gray truck pulling a small, tarped trailer came into sight, and Maxwell surged to his feet. Forget dinner. Eryn was here! Oh, and her dad. Never forget the father.

He closed the laptop and set it on the end table. He'd

need to move that if Tate and Stephanie came with the boys, since Jamie was endlessly curious and would certainly *not* leave it alone.

Maxwell strode across the great room, past the vacant registration desk to the main doors, which he flung open just as Eryn's car came to a stop behind her father's truck. It had been nine days since he'd seen her. Had he really kept count?

Keith slid out of the cab, smile wide as the Montana sky as he looked around. "So, this is Sweet River Ranch. I was hoping you weren't pulling my leg, boy."

"Never, sir. Welcome!" Maxwell's long legs ate the distance to Eryn's car, and he opened the door for her. "You made it! Hope you had a good drive? Did you enjoy Yellowstone?" Those texts had contained minimal information.

Keith stretched both arms in the air then bent from one side to the other. "Those geysers were amazing! I bet you visit every chance you get."

Maxwell scratched his neck. "Yeah… I haven't ever been, but I need to. Soon."

"Never been?" The man looked taken aback. "It's so close."

"Dad's right," Eryn offered with a smile as she exited the car. "You should see it."

Was this where Maxwell explained the definition of a workaholic? Nah, that could come later. "Definitely. It's on my list. I'm glad you enjoyed it, though."

"We spent all day yesterday in the park. That way we didn't have to pay to sleep there."

This girl needed to live a little. But… maybe, so did he.

"Well, you're here now." Maxwell gestured to take in the view. "This is the main lodge, as you can see. It contains the kitchen and dining hall as well as the offices. There are also guest rooms — basically, hotel rooms — on the second floor. You're welcome to a couple of those tonight, or you can move right into your duplex. Whichever you prefer. Either way, the dinner gong goes off at 5:30, and you can meet the skeleton staff then."

The two exchanged a look.

Keith hitched his pants. "Might as well unload now, I guess. We haven't got that much with us, honestly. Got rid of most everything in Kansas."

"Sure. We've got time. Let me round up a couple of guys to help."

"Oh, that's not necessary. It won't take Eryn and me but a few minutes. Just point us in the right direction."

Maxwell chuckled. "That's not how we do things here. We're a team. Bryce and Jordan are around and waiting for my call." Actually, he'd asked Jordan, but his brother had overheard. Hopefully Bryce wouldn't come on to Eryn too strong. The guy couldn't be trusted around women. Should Maxwell warn her?

He pulled out his phone, tapped a text to them both, and repocketed the device. "They'll meet us there. I'll grab one of the golf carts and lead the way to Hummingbird Lane."

Keith's eyebrows hiked up. "Hummingbird Lane?"

"Yep." Maxwell chuckled. "The ranch's former owners named the roads for winged creatures. We've got them all: Dragonfly Lane, Ladybug Lane, Wingfeather Lane... and the riding stables are on Pegasus. That's just a sampling."

The other man laughed as he shook his head and glanced at his daughter. "Whole 'nother world, right, Rynie?"

Eryn offered a shy smile. "It sure is."

"I hope it's a world you'll be glad you came to."

"I'm sure it will be."

He was going to do his best to make certain. "Okay, well, follow me. It's only another quarter mile or so." He jumped on a golf cart, drove toward the staff duplexes on Hummingbird, and parked in front of #4.

Keith smoothly backed the trailer in, a skill he'd learned with farm equipment, no doubt. Good sign.

"Welcome, Eryn." Maxwell opened her car door and indicated the right-hand door to the cedar-sided building. "Your temporary home sweet home."

"It's cute."

No one had ever said that before. The duplexes had been a cheap, quick build ten years back and were already showing their age. Maxwell and his grandfather had been discussing options. Yeah, maybe it was going to be quite a while before all the Sweet River projects were complete.

"It's small, is what it is." He opened the door and let her precede him inside. "They're all the same design and are more like glorified motel rooms than apartments, but that's okay, since no one needs to cook here."

The all-in-one living, dining room, and kitchen came first, with a bedroom and bathroom tucked beneath the loft. "There are staff laundry facilities down the lane. This time of year, the machines are usually vacant. In summer, you'll need to sign up for slots. Except the farmhouse has its own washer and dryer, so never mind."

She smiled at him then glanced behind him as her dad entered. "What do you think, Dad?"

Keith looked around, nodding. "Looks good for now." He reached a hand to shake Maxwell's. "I can't thank you enough for coming along at the exact right time with this offer. I'd been praying the good Lord would direct our paths like it says in Proverbs 3, and He came through, loud and clear."

"It's not every day a man gets to be an answer to prayer. I'm glad it worked out."

"Yo, you're here! Let the party begin!"

And now Maxwell got to introduce his brother to Eryn and her dad. Hopefully she wouldn't be enthralled by Bryce like half the female staff seemed to be.

The other half ignored Bryce or laughed in his face. That was the best-case scenario with Eryn.

How was this her life?

Eryn climbed the ladder to the loft and looked around in amazement. The duplex was not that fancy, but it was temporary.

The trip here, however, had been awe-inspiring. The mountains were a thousand times more majestic up close than in photos she'd seen. The geysers in Yellowstone were unbelievably impressive. And now here they were, her and Dad, a half-hour drive up a paved mountain road with a small lake glinting between enormous trees, some of which were already turning color at the beginning of October.

She'd only had a glimpse of the expansive log lodge

with its wide windows and a welcoming deck with Adirondack chairs and even a swing. To think she lived here now! Worked here.

Best of all was Maxwell Sullivan. She'd never be able to repay him for this opportunity as long as she lived. She'd be employed by his family and, yes, he'd hinted at a relationship last weekend, but men like him didn't date lowly employees. Kitchen staff.

She wouldn't get her hopes up on that account, but coming to Sweet River was still the experience of a lifetime. She'd make the most of it, and if Dad did well operating the farm side, it would remain a place she could retreat to even after she moved on herself.

But no thinking about that now, not while voices from outside on the stoop made her realize they had company. Must be the guys Maxwell had asked to help them unload… which only meant more people would be privy to the few shabby belongings they'd brought. There was no hiding that.

This loft would likely be her room, as Dad probably wouldn't want to climb the ladder multiple times a day at his age. A previous tenant had rigged a makeshift curtain to offer some privacy from the main floor. It would do.

"Eryn? Can you tell everyone where to put things?" Dad called.

"Coming right down." She turned and descended the ladder only to find a man standing right at the bottom to help her off. Not that she needed assistance. "Oh!"

"Hi. I'm Bryce, Maxwell's bigger and better-looking brother." He lifted her hand to his lips.

She jerked it away and stepped aside. "I'm Eryn."

The other stranger chuckled. "I'm Jordan, and I work for Max. Pleased to meet you, Eryn, and welcome to Sweet River Ranch."

"Thank you." She gave an irritated look at Bryce before turning to Dad.

Maxwell stood beside Dad, his eyes crinkling in amusement. "Sorry about my brother."

Eryn felt like shaking her fingers out, but that might be offensive. She might have to work with Bryce and didn't need an enemy. But she'd be keeping an eye on him, for sure. The guy didn't seem trustworthy.

"Dad, the main floor bedroom is smaller than the loft, but I'm not sure you want to access yours by a ladder? You pick, and I'll take the other space."

"You can have the loft, if you don't mind. I don't have that much stuff, and that will give you room for your sewing machine and such. Is that okay?"

"Sure. We won't be here that long, so I probably don't need it out, but it's fine, either way."

Maxwell clapped his hands at the others. "Start hauling, boys."

"Yes, boss." Bryce saluted as he winked at Eryn. "I don't know if you have any brothers, but in my experience, they're all like this."

"Bryce." Maxwell's voice held warning.

"I have no brothers." Why she felt she needed to even respond, she couldn't have said.

"This one is marked kitchen." Jordan set a box on the small Formica table. "I assume we can figure much of this out."

"Thank you." And she heaved a sigh of relief as Bryce followed Jordan back outside.

Dad disappeared into the bathroom, leaving Maxwell beside her.

"Sorry about my brother. He thinks he's God's gift to women."

Eryn suppressed her shudder. "Well, I might disagree."

"Good." Maxwell grinned, his gaze meeting and holding hers. "I'd hate to have to take him out. But I would, if I had to."

"Oh?" Her voice seemed devoid of breath.

"I want to get to know you better, like I said in Kansas."

"Me?"

Maxwell made a show of looking around the room. "I don't see anyone else I might be talking to."

"But we're here because you offered my father a job. A fresh start."

"And that offer was made because of you. Oh, he definitely qualifies for it. Don't get me wrong. But you're the real reason."

Maxwell was just as forward as his brother. Only, he was a whole lot more palatable.

And Eryn was mighty glad to be here to see where this might lead.

CHAPTER NINE

Maxwell loved the more intimate feeling of the dining hall in the offseason. Sure, he loved the buzz and activity of tourists over the summer, but this was more like extended family. He'd forged his own path for eight years, only tapping into the family dynamic when he had time, whatever that was, but reconnecting with his brothers and cousins had been more satisfying than he'd thought possible. Even Bryce.

He'd nearly said no to Grandfather's request, but the photos of neglected and half-finished guest cottages had lured him in. Good thing, too.

"Aunt Nadine, I'd like you to meet your new helper, Eryn Ralston, and her dad, Keith."

Nadine smiled over the dinner counter. "I'm happy to meet you, Eryn. It's not super busy this time of year, but I'll be glad to have an assistant, nonetheless."

Eryn offered a shy smile. "Do you want me to start tonight?"

"Heavens, no, child! Take a few days to settle in. Monday is soon enough."

"But—" Eryn's wide eyes appealed to Maxwell.

He touched her back. "What she says. If she needed you earlier, she'd say so."

"But—"

Keith reached across the counter and shook Nadine's hand. "I'm pleased to meet you."

"Likewise."

Wait, was Aunt Nadine blushing? Nah, couldn't be.

"Please dish yourselves up and find a seat out there." She fluttered a hand.

Maxwell nudged Eryn in front of him as they scooped pasta, sauce, and salad onto their plates then added garlic toast on the side. He glanced back at his aunt.

She was watching Keith but noticed Maxwell's smirk. Her face pinked, and she turned back into the kitchen.

Maxwell shook his head and set his tray down on a vacant table. Soon the three of them were settled with their food.

"Have your aunt and uncle been here at the ranch long?" Keith dipped his garlic toast into the sauce.

"My aunt and unc—" Maxwell cut himself off and managed not to laugh. "There's a whole story there, but the short answer is that Aunt Nadine's husband passed away before I could meet him. He's been gone several years."

"I'm sorry." But Keith's contemplative glance back to the kitchen mocked his words.

"The longer version is that my grandfather had an affair with his secretary before he met and married my grandmother. His secretary left Chicago without a forwarding address, and it wasn't so easy to track people back then. Anyway, Nadine had been searching for her father all her life, but her mother refused to divulge the man's name. Enter twenty-first century DNA testing and genealogy websites, and Nadine pinned my grandfather down with the evidence he was her father."

Eryn gaped at him as she lowered her laden fork to her plate. "That's crazy."

"It is, you're right. That's when Grandfather bought this ranch. He invited his daughter to work for him, and all us boys — my brothers, my cousin Graham, me — and Nadine's sons, our newfound cousins. Jude is away in Chicago right now at flight school, and Weston will be your boss, Keith. He's in charge of the stables and nominally oversees the farm operations as well."

"So, she's single?"

That's what Keith Ralston got out of the story? "Yes, she is."

"I see." The man looked thoughtful as he ate a meatball. "She's a good cook."

"Most everything is from scratch. She even bakes all the bread we go through around here." Maxwell smiled at Eryn. "She and her staff, of course."

"I've never baked bread." Eryn bit her lip and glanced toward the kitchen.

"I hear she's a good mentor." He touched Eryn's hand. "She won't expect you to know how to do everything the first day."

"I hope I won't disappoint her."

"Not possible." Okay, maybe he was coming on a little too much like Bryce, but Eryn's self-esteem seemed exceptionally low. Was it her personality? Did her father put her down? Maxwell hadn't seen any evidence of that, but he hadn't spent a lot of time with either of them, let alone together.

He was going to remedy that.

"Keith Ralston?" Weston stood beside the table with a tray in his hand, Paisley beside him.

"Yes, sir." Keith swallowed his bite, surged to his feet, and held out his hand.

"I'm Weston Kline, and this is my fiancée, Paisley Teele." He glanced at Maxwell as he shook Keith's hand. "I hear you're taking over Joseph's position. May we have a seat?"

Maxwell nodded and managed not to smile too wide. Weston was acting like a civilized human being for once in his life, not the sour grump everyone had grown used to since they'd met a year and a half ago. Paisley's doing, for sure. Oh, and God's.

"Paisley, this is Keith's daughter, Eryn. She'll be working with Nadine in the kitchen for now."

"I'm so happy to meet you!" Paisley gushed. "You're going to love it here. You're from Kansas?"

"Yes." Eryn offered a shy smile. "I've never been out west before."

"Oh, there's so much to do and see! I run the family activities here at the resort. We do trail rides and archery and kayaking and bonfires and all sorts of events. I hope you'll take advantage of everything that sounds interesting to you. I can hook you up with any of it."

"Thank you, but I'm not sure how all that fits around my work schedule."

"There are fewer families here during the school year,

but we do things on weekends still through Thanksgiving. And then we have big events planned for Christmas week. Not kayaking so much." Paisley giggled.

"No, we'll be at least knee-deep in snow by then." Maxwell chuckled. "But it's not too cold for kayaking now, if you enjoy being on the water."

"I've never been." Eryn seemed to shrink in on herself. "Any of those things, really."

"Hey, you went trail-riding in Kansas," Maxwell chided gently. "We could ride here, too."

"Oh, let's!" Paisley brightened. "Tomorrow afternoon? Maxwell, you up for that?"

"Sound good, Eryn?"

Eryn glanced toward her father, who was deep in conversation with Weston. Maxwell heard references to pregnant heifers and silage and the fence on the west pasture before tuning them back out.

"I don't want to be a bother." Eryn poked her fork at her plate.

"You're not. We look for any excuse to go riding around here. Which horse for her, do you think, Maxwell?"

"Mirage, probably. I'll take Nutmeg or whichever one needs exercise most."

"Sounds good. Let's plan to head out right after lunch. You'll love the back country, Eryn. It's so beautiful here."

"You're staying this winter then, Paisley?" he asked.

She flushed. "Of course! I have a wedding to plan!"

"Are you guys getting married here at the lodge?"

"Yes. Stephanie and Tate's and Cadence and Graham's were so beautiful here." She turned to Eryn. "Imagine the bride descending the log staircase over there—" she pointed "—and the groom waiting by the fireplace. There's room for almost one hundred guests, not that Weston and I know that many people."

"Only the entire staff at Sweet River." Maxwell chuckled.

"Not everyone needs to attend the ceremony. We'll have a big reception and dance out on the lawn afterward."

Eryn's eyes widened as she absorbed Paisley's plans.

Maxwell could relate. Paisley's enthusiasm was a bit much at times, but she'd worn Weston's reserves down.

Unfair. Weston had come into his own with the light of Paisley's love shining on him.

Maxwell wasn't the recluse his cousin had been. He didn't need a woman to bring out the best in him. But... maybe he did.

Or maybe it was the other way around. Maybe Eryn needed someone who believed in her the way Paisley had believed in Weston.

Could Maxwell be that someone? Did he even want to be? While he'd occasionally thought of getting serious with Heather, she'd come to him as an equal with her strong personality and opinions.

Eryn would agree with everything anyone said if she wasn't sure how her opinions would be taken. Was he the right person to help her instill confidence and stand her ground?

Did he want to be?

ERYN LISTENED to the other woman bubble on and on about her upcoming wedding to the cowboy, who was completely ignoring her and focused on answering Dad's questions about the ranch operations.

Obviously, Paisley didn't take that lack of attention as negative. Maybe no one dared ignore her for long. She seemed like a woman who got what she wanted.

Eryn didn't even know what she wanted, let alone how to forge her own path to achieve it. Was Sweet River Ranch a place where she could figure all that out?

If not here, where? If not now, when? She was 28 years old, and she'd existed in her sister's shadow since birth. Amelia had been the healthy twin who learned to crawl and walk before sickly Eryn caught up. How could Eryn possibly still feel Amelia's shadow all these years later? Her sister had never been to Montana. No one here knew her except Dad.

And Maxwell.

Eryn had read a few more snippets of Amelia's journal in which she gushed about adolescent Maxwell, reliving every interaction between them. Maybe by the 2010 diaries, Amelia would be on to some other boy. Eryn could hardly wait to find out, because the descriptions and anecdotes were killing her with jealousy.

She only had a crush on him now because he was the first man in her entire life to make any attempt to draw her out. That was all. He'd never be truly interested in a wallflower like her. Not if he'd been a fraction as interested in the juvenile version of Amelia as she had been of him.

No, she'd have a front-row seat here of him falling in love with some other woman. Maybe someday it would be her turn for romance. At least the ranch seemed more possible for that than Gilead, where everyone had known the twins since birth.

She glanced surreptitiously around the dining room. There were several tables with only men and several with only women as well as some with mixed groups. How many employees stayed over the winter?

"What do you think, Eryn?"

She gave her head a little shake and looked at Paisley. "Pardon me? I missed what you said." She'd have to do a better job of focusing.

"You must be tired after days on the road. My nosy questions can keep." Paisley nudged Maxwell. "Is tomorrow a date, or are you too busy?"

"A ride sounds great. I'm caught up with the projects for now. Janessa says we're waiting on the flooring for the next three cottages. Something about the vinyl planks we need being temporarily out-of-stock. She figures they'll be available Friday."

Eryn hadn't even stopped to wonder about what Maxwell did at the ranch or that he might work with women. Women who were probably more attractive and fun than she was. Maybe he was even in a relationship.

No, that couldn't be right, or he wouldn't have hinted the way he had in Kansas, like he might be interested in her.

Dad turned to her. "Weston says we can have a look at the farmhouse tomorrow after lunch."

Paisley slung her arm over Weston's shoulder. "Can you make that later in the afternoon? I invited Eryn and Maxwell to go riding with us then."

The serious-looking cowboy covered his fiancée's hand with his. His whole demeanor softened as he looked at her. "It won't take long to swing by Joseph's. We can still be on the trail by two. Sound okay?"

"Okaaay." Paisley dragged out the word and batted her eyelashes at Weston. "There's still plenty of daylight."

Weston nodded at Maxwell then at Eryn. "That's a plan, then. Joseph and Marie won't move out until after Thanksgiving. When I gave that extension, I didn't realize we'd be able to fill his position so quickly. On the plus side, it means you can work with him for a while and learn the ropes. I'm far more active with the horses than with the cattle, so this works out well."

"Will you be living at the farmhouse, Eryn?" Paisley asked. "Or in staff housing?"

"I… I didn't realize I had options."

"The farmhouse is old, but it's homier than the duplexes. If it were me, I'd stick with my dad." She grimaced. "If I had a father worth sticking with."

Eryn's eyebrows rose.

Paisley shook her head. "Long story. I'm a bit jealous of your relationship, that's all. Let's leave it at that for today."

Maxwell elbowed Paisley's arm lightly. "Let her see the options before she makes a decision."

"Of course. I wasn't trying to push her. But I'm talking too much again, right?" Paisley wrinkled her nose. "I always talk too much."

Maxwell's eyes crinkled as he grinned at Eryn. "I'm not sure about *too much,* but it's a lot, right, Eryn?"

"Not too much at all." Eryn smiled at Paisley. She hadn't had a good friend in forever. Maybe she and Paisley could hang out some. Then again, the other woman was planning a wedding, and she probably would have her own friends in place to help with that. She was just the sort who was friendly with everyone.

"Anyone want more garlic toast? There are only a few pieces left." Nadine stood between Dad and Weston at the table. She carried a platter and held out a piece of toast with a pair of tongs.

"Thanks, Mom." Weston held out his plate as she set one on it.

"How about you, Keith?"

"Uh, sure. Th-thank you."

Eryn blinked. Dad, stammering?

"How about the rest of you?" Nadine looked between them.

"Yes, please," Maxwell and Paisley said at the same time.

Eryn shook her head and murmured, "No, thanks." Too much was going on around her for her to absorb. More food in her unsettled gut wouldn't help.

CHAPTER TEN

W atch closely. Soon you'll be tacking up on your own." Maxwell winked at her.

"Okay." Eryn bit her lip. Was he brushing her off? She shouldn't have read so much into his attentiveness so far. Truth was, she wasn't sure she'd want to ride horseback without him nearby. Or did the other women sometimes go as a group? Would she make the sort of friends here who'd invite her along?

Besides Paisley, that is. Paisley had talked to a bunch more people before Weston had finally dragged her out of the dining hall last night. It had happened again at lunchtime. What must it be like to be so outgoing and confident? Eryn wasn't likely to ever find out.

Maxwell slipped the bit into Mirage's mouth and worked the leather over her ears. The mare shook her blond mane, but not as though she were annoyed by the straps.

Was the man crooning to the horse?

Eryn tilted her head to hear better. It sure sounded like the soft humming came from Maxwell. Huh.

He reached for a soft pad and placed it on Mirage's back then swung a worn-looking saddle over, explaining the placement and adjustment of the bands as he did so.

How was she supposed to remember all these steps? Especially when Maxwell smiled at her like that?

Playing dumb wasn't in her wheelhouse, though. She'd learn how to do this herself unless the opportunity simply never came up again. That was most likely. She'd be busy in the kitchen while others went out on the trails.

"Okay, remember how to mount up? Left foot here — we're going to need to get you a pair of boots in Jewel Lake next trip down."

He stood so close as he held Mirage in place. "Boots? I hardly think I'll be riding often enough to need them."

"I should talk to Tate about making new boots part of the official staff clothing issue when newcomers join us." Maxwell winked at her as though sharing a joke. "This is Montana, after all."

She tucked her sneaker-clad foot into the stirrup and grabbed onto the saddle horn. As she hesitated, taking a moment to visualize the motion sequence he'd shown her last time, his hands rested lightly on her waist.

"Ready? Up you go."

She bounced lightly and swung into the saddle. It felt effortless with Maxwell's assistance.

He looked up at her. "Good job! You did that like a pro, not like someone who's only ridden once before."

"Thanks for helping." She smiled shyly at him as she gathered the reins as he'd shown her in Kansas.

"No problem." Maxwell still stood beside Mirage's head, focused on Eryn.

She tore her gaze away. "Which horse are you riding?"

He blinked and stepped back. "Nutmeg."

"I got her tacked for you, dude." Weston's voice came from the alley. "You guys ready to go? Paisley's itching for a run. She has Enchantment and Ranger out in the corral already."

"Ready." Eryn lightly pressed her knees against Mirage's ribs as Maxwell had explained last time. The mare walked out behind Weston. Behind her, she could hear the creak of Maxwell's saddle as he mounted up, then the clomp-clomp as his horse came behind her.

Weston opened the gate and Paisley led them through before he closed it and mounted his huge horse with the kind of ease Eryn could never hope for.

This felt more like a real trail ride than at Walker Ridge. There, it had been a reunion activity in which many of her former classmates had participated. Here it was more like... a date. But that was silly. Maxwell was just helping her settle in. Besides, the outing had been Paisley's idea, not his.

"Isn't it beautiful?" Maxwell spoke from beside her as Paisley and Weston took the lead.

"It really is. There are so many shades of fall colors. They're so vibrant."

"I love the smell of the forest, too. The fir trees and spruce."

Eryn sniffed. "And... vanilla?"

Maxwell brightened. "That's the sweetgrass the ranch is

named for. It grows in low-lying areas like over there near the lake." He pointed left of the trail.

"I've heard of it. It grows in parts of Kansas, too, but not near Gilead that I know of."

"It blooms in spring, and the fragrance is strongest after rains. Now it's drying on the stem, and that has its own aroma. The indigenous peoples used it for medicinal and ceremonial purposes."

"It smells lovely. I can see where it got its name." Eryn mulled it for a moment. "Is it protected?"

"Protected?" Maxwell shifted in his saddle as he looked at her. "You mean like endangered? Not at all. It's hardy and grows everywhere. Why?"

"I was just wondering." Should she tell him her idea? He could only agree or laugh, right? "I thought it might make nice sachets for linen closets."

"Smart thought!" He looked at her with admiration. "We could sell them in the gift shop."

"There's a gift shop?" She'd noticed a sign inside the lodge, but no evidence one actually existed.

"It's closed over the winter. We've never really gotten it going well, though. A local potter has some items there, but honestly, it's mostly full of leftover trinkets from the ranch's previous owners."

"There's a lot you could do with the Sweet River name. It would just take some brainstorming and creativity."

He chuckled. "Do I hear a volunteer? Because no one has been inspired thus far."

Eryn stared at him until he turned to look at her again.

"What are you looking at me like that for?"

"Volunteer?"

He shook his head slightly, clearly not understanding. "We pay a manager, of course, but even that hasn't been a great fit. You want the job? Tell Tate about your ideas. He'd probably let you run with it."

"You said volunteer." She'd probably be too busy working in the kitchen to take on unpaid projects, but that was only part-time for the winter.

"I meant some of our staff kind of pick the area they'd like to work. I didn't mean it would be gratis on top of your regular job."

"But I was hired for the kitchen."

"That's part-time only and, uh…" Maxwell scratched the back of his neck.

"And what?" she asked suspiciously.

"Aunt Nadine doesn't really need help, though she's happy to have it."

Eryn's gut clenched. "You hired me for a nonexistent job?"

He grimaced. "Not that exactly. There will be plenty to do, but don't feel like you need to stay in the kitchen unless you love it there."

Clarity formed. "You offered me a job because you wanted my dad to come."

"Well, yes, at first, but—"

Eryn kneed Mirage's sides, and the mare shifted into a trot. Eryn clung to the saddle horn at the horse's jolting stride.

"Whoa." Hoofbeats came alongside, and Maxwell reached for Mirage's bridle to slow her. "Easy, girl."

Eryn glared at Maxwell. "Leave her. I'll stay on. You don't need to patronize me."

"Patronize?" His brows furrowed. "What are you talking about?"

"I thought you offered me... never mind." She urged Mirage faster again. Paisley and Weston were just ahead. They couldn't be too far up the trail.

"Eryn, wait." Maxwell came up beside her again. "You think I offered you a job so that your father would take over the farming here?"

"That's what you said." She shot daggers at him with her eyes.

"That's backwards." He shook his head. "I offered *him* a job so *you* would come."

Her body slacked as her mouth gaped. She only realized it when she began to slip off Mirage's back.

ERYN WAS SLIDING IN SLO-MO, her eyes widening with panic.

Maxwell leaped out of Nutmeg's saddle to catch her before she tumbled onto the hard trail. Or, more likely, caught her sneaker in the stirrups. She all but fell into his arms.

"Hey, I've got you. Are you okay?" He held her while she found her balance.

"Um, yes. I can't believe I fell off."

"I was happy to catch you." He was still holding her, her long blond hair brushing his arms. And not all the vanilla scent came from the sweetgrass. Some of it came from Eryn, but he could manage not to sniff her, right? Barely.

"I'm sorry." She straightened and stepped aside. "Wow, the horses are still standing right here."

"Not much fazes them. They're used to greenhorns."

"That's good, I guess." She dusted off her jeans, not meeting his gaze. "Sorry about that."

"Eryn."

She glanced at him then away. "Yes?"

"You seem startled that I want to get to know you."

"I guess... why?"

He blinked. "Why wouldn't I want to get to know you? You're beautiful. You're strong. You're smart. You're—"

"I'm not Amelia. That was her, not me."

"I know you're not Amelia." How did Eryn mean that, anyway? She and her twin weren't the least bit alike in looks or personality, so why would she think he'd be confused as to which was which?

"Everyone liked her." She snuck him a furtive glance. "*You* liked her."

Maxwell scoffed lightly. "When we were 13, but did we ever date? Nope. I never asked her out."

"But..."

The mares both grazed along the trail and didn't seem like they were too anxious about this impromptu rest stop. "What kind of 'but,' Eryn? I didn't go out with her or anyone else. I was too focused on finishing high school and getting out of Gilead." Ugh. That didn't put him in the greatest light. Still, it was the truth. "I haven't been involved since then, either. A few casual dates with friends for special events, but my heart has never been involved."

Until now. But there was no way she was ready to hear that. He was barely ready to acknowledge it to himself.

There was something about Eryn Ralston that had snuck past his defenses. He'd pretended he was only helping someone who needed a leg up, but it was more. Way more.

"Never?"

She looked so vulnerable that he wanted to take her in his arms and kiss her. Reassure her.

Maxwell backed up a step. That was an impulse that couldn't be acted upon. Not yet, not without careful fore-thought. Making sure he was ready for some sort of commitment.

Making sure she was.

He held her gaze. "I never met anyone I wanted to get to know in that way. Until now."

Her blue eyes widened. "Me?"

"You." Maxwell nodded. "I asked you at the reunion if we could get to know each other. That wasn't a casual line I'd toss out to just anyone. In fact, I had never used it before."

Eryn shook her head slightly, still meeting his gaze. "But you lived in Montana, and I lived in Kansas. It was... never going to work." Her voice grew breathless as she finished speaking.

"When I heard about your dad's situation, I knew I could help, and I wanted to. And the side benefit was that I hoped you'd come, too. So, then we'd both live here, in Montana. On the same ranch."

She blinked and looked around as though seeing the forest for the first time. "I... this is crazy. I can't believe I uprooted my entire life and moved over a thousand miles away. I can't believe *Dad* did."

Maxwell wanted to ask her if she'd noticed Keith's reaction to Weston's mother, but it might be too early for that kind of speculation, both for the older folks, but also for him and Eryn.

"I don't think he regrets it," Maxwell said at last. "He seems happy for the new opportunity."

"That house is cute, too. Nicer than our house on the farm."

"It's been well kept," Maxwell agreed.

"It's all so overwhelming."

He wanted to ask her for a date, but maybe he'd wait a few days before springing that on her. He might have upended his life on a whim several times over, but she was clearly uncomfortable with the big move she and her father had undertaken.

Soon, though.

The sound of hoofbeats coming back down the trail had him reaching for their horses' reins.

Paisley's horse skidded to a stop first. "Oh, there you are. We just realized we'd lost sight of you."

Maxwell stifled a snort. That pair had been so wrapped up in each other's eyes as they trotted out, he doubted they'd remembered for five seconds that they'd invited him and Eryn along.

"Is everything okay?" Weston asked.

"We're good. Minor mishap." Maxwell turned back to Eryn. "Want to keep going?"

She gave him a shy smile. "Sure."

He boosted her into the saddle, unable to keep the smile off of his own face as he mounted Nutmeg. "Lead on. We're right behind you this time."

CHAPTER ELEVEN

D ad ushered Eryn into the foyer of Creekside Fellowship on Sunday morning. Attending church wasn't required for Sweet River staff, but it seemed expected for those who weren't on duty.

"Good morning! I'm Eli Bryson, the youth pastor here, and this is my wife, Harper." The young man reached out to shake Dad's hand.

"Keith Ralston and my daughter, Eryn. We just moved here from Kansas to work at Sweet River Ranch."

The beautiful blonde on Eli's arm beamed at Eryn. "It's a big change for you, but you're going to love it here. I grew up in Atlanta, so this was a bit of a culture shock for me."

"A bit?" Eli laughed at his wife.

"Okay, a lot." Harper winked at Eryn. "And it will soon be winter again, but you're probably used to blizzards from Kansas."

Eli grinned and shook his head. "You haven't experienced a true blizzard yet, love. Just a bit of snow."

"A *bit of snow* that gets neck-deep and takes out the power lines." She gave him a mock glare.

Dad chuckled. "We get some snow and a lot of wind in Kansas. Maxwell told us to expect more snow but less wind, in general."

"Sounds right." Eli checked his watch. "The service is about to begin, so we should find our seats. Our senior pastor, Marshall Smith, is preaching today. I hope you'll enjoy his sermon and be challenged as well. Good to meet you."

"We'll have to get together." Harper fluttered her fingers at Eryn as she tucked her hand in the crook of her husband's elbow then turned away.

A gorgeous woman like Harper, married to a pastor, wouldn't follow through on that, but it was a nice, welcoming gesture.

Welcoming guitar and piano music flowed from the sanctuary as Eryn stepped through the doors from the foyer.

"There's a couple of seats," Dad whispered, gesturing to their right.

Eryn slipped in, only to realize she sat beside Nadine with Weston and Paisley beyond. She flashed a quick smile. "Hi."

Dad leaned past her to shake Nadine's hand, then Weston's. He'd probably have reached for Paisley's if he could, but the worship leader invited everyone to stand and sing the opening song, "Come, Now Is the Time to Worship."

A pang of nostalgia slammed Eryn, memories of Fount of Grace Fellowship back home with Mom standing between Amelia and her to keep them from poking at each other. The Gilead worship team was more professional than here, more polished. That probably had something to do with the music track at the Bible college. Many students in the preaching and drama pathways also participated in Sunday morning services onstage.

Creekside Fellowship was a small-town church with a western flair, with a lot of people wearing jeans and sweatshirts. Eryn smoothed her floral skirt and tugged at the hem of her pastel pink sweater as she furtively glanced around. The only woman who looked more dressed up had been the youth pastor's stunning wife.

Also, she'd missed most of the song. A portly middle-aged man took the platform and offered an opening prayer before the worship leader invited them all to sing once again. There were new songs and old favorites. Maybe it wasn't that different from back home.

Was Gilead still home? She pushed that thought out of her head as she tried to focus on the worshipful lyrics.

Then her gaze caught on a row of Sullivans off to the side. Maxwell with his wavy hair sat between his brothers, his three-year-old nephew snuggled into his lap.

Aww. Was there anything sweeter than seeing a big, tough guy holding a little kid like it was no big deal? Not that Maxwell was big. He was more on the wiry side, but the tough part of the label fit. The man had muscles that went for miles, probably from all the power tools and building materials he handled.

She'd love to watch him at work sometime, but that might be construed as creepy. Besides, she'd be confined to the kitchen... except he'd hinted that if she had an interest in the resort's gift shop, a transfer could be arranged.

The sweetgrass sachets were a no-brainer, and she'd looked up the native grass to discover it was also used for basket-weaving and other crafts. So... a section for sweetgrass.

Then, just plain sweets to keep playing on the ranch name. Locally made candy? She'd do some research and see if that existed.

Local pottery was a nice start, but there were probably other artisans, too. Maybe someone who created stained glass designs or landscape paintings or carved horses or...

"All God's promises are yes and amen, according to the Bible. That means if He says it, He will do it. Period."

Eryn blinked at the man in the pulpit. Oh, dear, she was woolgathering like crazy instead of paying attention in church.

God's promises. Check. There were many of them in scripture. She should make a study of them... or maybe that's what Pastor Marshall was on about?

She slipped the bulletin from Dad's lap and scanned the sermon information inside. Hmm. Looked like part three of a longer series on covenant promises. She'd do better to focus on Pastor Marshall's words than to let her mind wander.

"We humans have our own timelines. We're like sweetgrass, blooming for a short while, then dying off, while God is eternal. Not only can He see a much bigger picture than we can, but He *created* that bigger picture so unfathomable to us temporary beings."

Wasn't that the truth? It wasn't even possible for humans to understand how little they understood.

"As a father has compassion on his children, so the Lord

has compassion on those who fear him; for he knows how we are formed, he remembers that we are dust. The life of mortals is like grass, they flourish like a flower of the field; the wind blows over it and it is gone, and its place remembers it no more." Pastor Marshall paused, holding up his Bible. "But from everlasting to everlasting the Lord's love is with those who fear him, and his righteousness with their children's children — with those who keep his covenant and remember to obey his precepts."

The pastor's gaze ranged the quiet sanctuary. "Psalm 103 is David's writing. He knew how insignificant he was, but he clung to God's promise of His loving, compassionate presence. The same God is still our God today, and we can know Him more fully than David ever could. We have the New Testament, which tells the story of how Jesus fulfilled the Law and the Prophets. David only glimpsed hints of that in a future mostly obscured from him. But we have it all right here."

Up went the leather-bound book once again. "We can read God's promises, and we can see how they have been accomplished. All of them? Not yet. But there is ample evidence to leave no room for doubt that God will fulfill the remainder as well."

Dad shifted restlessly beside Eryn, but a surreptitious glance his direction revealed his rapt attention focused on the pastor.

What was he finding so fascinating in this sermon? The same thing as her?

"Hey, would you two like to join us for lunch?" Maxwell had made his way toward Eryn and her dad so quickly after the benediction that he still held his nephew, Jamie. "We're headed to the Golden Grill down near the lakefront."

Aunt Nadine turned to Eryn. "Oh, you should go. You need to experience their food and ambience."

Maxwell chuckled. "Or you could head back to the ranch and reheat a bowl of chili Nadine left in the walk-in cooler. It's great chili, but you'll have plenty of chances to experience it over the winter."

"Are you saying my menu is repetitive?" Aunt Nadine swatted at his arm, but the grin on her face gave her away.

"In the best way," he assured her then turned back to Eryn. "My treat."

"Oh, you don't have to do that," Dad protested. "The ranch provided us with a larger relocation allowance than we needed. We can pick up our own tab."

Then it would feel less like a date… which was probably for the best. Still, Eryn eyed Maxwell a little warily. What was that about? He wasn't all that experienced at wooing women, but he hadn't thought it would be this hard to gain trust once he'd made up his mind.

Bryce didn't seem to have any trouble getting women on the same page, at least temporarily. Wally had married his high-school sweetheart.

Tate, like Maxwell, had been somewhat reclusive before he'd met Stephanie, but their relationship had shot into outer space in the blink of an eye, and they'd married within a couple of months of meeting. Made Maxwell feel like a sluggard. After all, he'd reconnected with Eryn a couple of weeks ago. Shouldn't they be practically engaged by now?

"That sounds nice." Eryn's quiet voice interrupted his thoughts.

His gaze swung to meet hers. She was on track with imminent engagement? No. Lunch. Lunch at the Golden Grill was on the agenda, not wedding bells. Maxwell needed to get his head in the game and focus on that whole one-step-at-a-time thing.

Hard to do. At work, he made and implemented snap decisions while juggling half a dozen subcontractors, often on more than one project at a time.

That decisiveness was not going to work with Eryn Ralston… even though it apparently had worked on Tate's wife. Or maybe Stephanie had done just as much pursuing as Tate had. They'd certainly been on the same page as far as speed went.

"Gamma Dean?" Jamie reached for Aunt Nadine.

"You sweet thing." Nadine plucked the boy from Maxwell's arms then turned toward Weston and Paisley. "See this adorable child? Don't take too long getting a few of these happening, okay?"

"Wedding isn't until spring, Mom." Weston rolled his eyes. "Hold your horses."

Paisley giggled. "But after that, look out!"

Maxwell chuckled. It was no secret that Paisley wanted a large family. He couldn't help but wonder how Weston would do with a bunch of noisy kids ripping around, but the cowboy had mellowed considerably since succumbing to Paisley's charms a few months back. Probably he'd be the disciplinarian and voice of reason to Paisley's indulgence. Or maybe not.

Maxwell turned to Keith. "You can follow my truck, or I can give you directions. It's not hard to find."

Weston grimaced. "Or just follow anyone from the church parking lot. Seems like most everyone is headed there."

"But not us today." Paisley batted her eyes at Weston as she leaned against him. "We're off to Missoula for the afternoon."

Maxwell shook his head at the smirk on his cousin's face. Who would ever have thought it? The dictionary might as well have had Weston's image beside its entry for grumpy before Paisley had won him over.

"Anyway." Maxwell turned back to Keith. "The Golden Grill faces the town square a block up from the beach. Can't wait to see you there." He reached back for Jamie. "Come on, bucko. Let me take you back to your parents."

"Are they coming, too?" Eryn asked softly.

"No, they usually go to Stephanie's parents' house for Sunday lunch. It's just Bryce and me today."

Eryn's nose wrinkled for a second, and Maxwell did a mental fist pump. That reaction wasn't one of attraction. For once, he was winning where Bryce was losing. Not that he was the least bit interested in any of the other women Bryce flirted with. This one, though? He'd fight his brother for her.

Jamie squished Maxwell's cheeks between his small palms and peered into his eyes.

Ouch. That hurt. "What, bucko?"

"Luff you Unc Max."

"I love you, too, kid." Had Eryn heard that exchange? He glanced at her to see a gentle smile as she looked between them. Yes! Another mental fist pump.

"See you in a few." He shifted Jamie to his hip.

"Are you going there for lunch, too?" he heard Keith ask as he walked away.

Wait, what?

"I was thinking of it, yes," Aunt Nadine replied.

"Maybe you could join us. If you don't have other plans."

"I'd like that."

Maxwell passed Jamie to Tate.

"What are you smirking about? Score a hot date?"

He chuckled. "If you mean, am I taking Eryn *and her father* for lunch at the Grill, then sure. But what is really catching my funny bone is Eryn's dad asking Aunt Nadine to join us."

Tate swung to look at the back of the church. "Say what?"

"I think it's cute."

"I'm not sure people in their fifties want to be thought cute if they're interested in each other. But are they, really?"

"Good point. And... yes, I think so. Time will tell."

Tate shook his head. "You are tempting me to ditch Arlys and Jack in favor of being a fly on the wall at the diner, but I'd never be forgiven. Gotta keep the in-laws happy."

"You say it as though you don't like them." Maxwell recalled some issues at first. Jack Simpson had been priming his daughter to marry a pastor for her entire life, and Eli Bryson in specific for a couple of years before Eli turned around and married Harper.

"We do okay now." Tate grinned. "The boys help, especially Simon, though they're pretty great with Jamie, too."

"I should be going."

Tate looked past him. "They're headed to the foyer, with Eryn behind Keith and Nadine."

"Should be interesting."

"Keep me updated, bro." Tate elbowed Maxwell. "On both developments."

Maxwell only hoped there'd be something to report.

CHAPTER TWELVE

Eryn slid into the large booth the middle-aged hostess ushered them into, Dad behind her. Across, Maxwell entered first, followed by his aunt, then his brother. She managed not to let her nose wrinkle at Bryce's wink. That guy was much too forward for her. Too slick. Too full of himself.

The hostess set down a stack of menus and glanced between them, her face alive with curiosity. "Welcome to the Golden Grill. What can I get you folks to drink?"

"Black coffee, please." Maxwell gestured to Eryn. "You?"

"Herbal tea?"

"Sure. We have chamomile and mint."

"Mint, please."

The others ordered, and Maxwell leaned toward her. "Don't let Paisley hear you order herbal tea."

Eryn widened her eyes. "Why's that?"

"She thinks Earl Grey is the only beverage that matters. She takes it strong and black."

"Oh." She smiled a little. "I'll be careful around her."

"Hey, I was teasing. You can order whatever you like, whether she's nearby or not. You do you."

"Okay." Of course, that's what he'd meant. He hadn't been making fun of her choice so much as making conversation. She opened the menu, aware of Dad chatting with Nadine and Bryce across the table. How did he do that so casually? But she could make an effort. "What's good here?"

"Everything." Maxwell chuckled. "Truly, you can't go wrong. I'm going for a cheeseburger and fries today."

Nadine elbowed him. "Where's your veggie, young man?"

Maxwell gave his aunt a hangdog look. "I'll eat extra at dinner?"

Nadine shook her head. "You boys. I'll order you each a side salad, you hear me? And you'll eat it, too."

"Yes'm." But Maxwell's wink was for Eryn. "You heard the sergeant, Eryn. Make sure whatever you order has a vegetable. Apparently, a wisp of lettuce and a slice of tomato doesn't count."

Nadine mock-glared at Maxwell as she closed her menu. He laughed.

Eryn smiled. Even though the aunt and her nephews hadn't known each other long, they seemed to have established a rapport.

The hostess returned with their drinks. "You must be new here." She placed Dad's coffee in front of him. "I'm Estelle. My husband and I own this diner."

"Keith Ralston and my daughter, Eryn. We've recently moved from Kansas."

"Well, I hope you enjoy Jewel Lake! It's a great little town, and there's always something going on."

Across the table, Maxwell's eyes danced with mirth, but he didn't say anything other than give his order when Estelle produced an order pad and pencil.

Nadine nudged him again.

Why didn't Eryn have an aunt like her? Wouldn't her life have been easier if either of her parents had siblings who might have taken an interest in her and her twin? Though Amelia likely wouldn't have cared. Or else, she'd have hogged the attention.

On the other hand, Eryn didn't want relatives to suddenly appear the way Maxwell had explained the Klines' arrival into the Sullivan clan. That would have been so unsettling.

A loud group of cowboys with women on their arms surrounded the long, makeshift table down the center of the café and took their seats.

"Be with you in a minute," Estelle hollered. "The usual drinks?"

"Yes, ma'am!" one of the cowboys called back.

"Those are the Cavanagh brothers," Maxwell said. "They run Rockstead Ranch just north of Sweet River." He chuckled. "And they own the middle of the Golden Grill for Sunday lunch."

Six men in jeans and plaid shirts hung their cowboy hats on a nearby coat tree and held chairs for their gorgeous women. The women looked casually elegant as they chatted amongst themselves even though they sat interspersed with their men.

What must it be like to marry into a ranching family like that? The Sullivans were different, since there were only three brothers plus their cousins.

A flush shot up Eryn's cheeks. She had no business thinking about Maxwell's family as though she had any connection to them. Sure, he hinted he wanted to date her, but that wouldn't last, would it?

At least, this time Amelia wasn't around to steal a potential boyfriend from under her nose. Eryn swallowed hard. Also, the potential boyfriend wasn't pretending to like Eryn so he could get closer to Amelia. That had been incredibly humiliating, enough to call Eryn off dating forever.

Or until her sister died. But the scars ran deep.

Bryce excused himself and pulled up a chair at the end of the Cavanagh table, where he laughed along with the cowboys at who knew what.

And then Eryn realized Maxwell was watching her again. She smiled at him pensively. Why couldn't she just relax and enjoy the attention while she had it? The sooner he figured out what a wallflower she was, the sooner he'd turn his attention elsewhere. Then she could go back to stitching quilts and listening to audiobooks and not dreaming at all of romance.

"Deep in thought?" he asked quietly.

"I guess so. Sorry I'm such poor company."

"People don't have to talk incessantly to be good company. In fact, that might ensure they're *not*."

She felt that way herself, but then, he seemed to be so much more outgoing than she was. She was nearly always afraid she'd say the wrong thing, and someone would make fun of her. Not Dad so much. Other people.

"So, you're starting in the kitchen tomorrow?"

Eryn nodded. "Yes. I'll be prepping in the morning. Does she really do it all herself?"

"No, she has a casual part-timer besides you, and help on weekends we're booked. You'll meet them over the next few days."

"Then... does she really need me?"

Maxwell grinned. "She was happy to have you join the team."

That wasn't the same thing as being needed.

"Have you been giving more thought to the gift shop? I'll show you what there is when we get back to the lodge if you like. It might be inspiring." He grimaced. "Or it might not be. No pressure, either way."

"I have thought a bit about it." She wasn't about to tell him that had mostly been during the sermon. "I'd like a tour, thank you." And more time with Maxwell was also welcome, especially if the focus wasn't on her.

"Perfect. We'll do that."

"Tell me more about what you do at the ranch."

"I'd given my crew a couple of weeks off over the reunion, and they've been trickling back over the weekend. We get back to work in the morning. Several cottages are nearing completion."

"I'd like to see that sometime."

"Deal. Maybe a bit later in the week, once we're back in the groove. There will almost certainly be a lot of little things needing my attention over the first few days as we get back to speed."

He'd brushed her off. But not completely. What he said made sense.

"We've got another set of cottages to work on over the

winter, but we're also nearing finality on the plans for eight treehouses to be built in spring." His grin reached his eyes. "Grandfather is calling the new road Eagles' Nest Lane to go along with the theme."

"Treehouses? For tourists?" Eryn's eyes widened.

"Yep. They're a thing, and we have a grove of larger trees north of the lake. We've been working on the environmental impact plans, and we've cleared every hurdle so far. Just a few more assessments to go before we can start laying out services to the area."

"Electricity?"

"And plumbing. They'll each have a bathroom up there."

"Wow. I didn't know that was possible."

"I've been working with an architect for the past few months now. It's all coming together." He grinned. "I thrive on making the impossible possible."

This guy. Was there any project he couldn't envision, pursue, and bring to completion?

MAXWELL UNLOCKED the door to the gift shop and flipped on the light switch before ushering Eryn inside. What would she think? The room wasn't large, but it had a bank of windows facing the deck along the front of the lodge, plus a smaller one beside the door to the foyer, which had been obscured with corrugated plastic for the winter.

He studied her as she turned slowly, taking in the shelves displaying trinkets, the rack on the back wall with a few books of local cowboy lore, and several empty tables.

Also, someone should periodically dust in here, even in

the offseason. He'd mention it to Kaci, the head housekeeper.

Finally, he couldn't stand it anymore. "What do you think?"

Eryn looked at him as she touched a plastic souvenir horse probably made overseas somewhere. "It… could use help."

Maxwell belted out a laugh. "You think?"

Eryn smiled. "Yes?"

"What would you do with this space if I handed it to you and asked you to create a gift shop for Sweet River?"

She pursed her lips.

He tried not to notice.

Eryn picked up the horse. "Do you really want to know?"

Maxwell leaned against the wall, his arms crossed over his chest. "Definitely. Hit me with it."

"Well, I'd start with getting rid of all this… junk. It's vaguely cowboyish, but it doesn't say anything about this place. Or about the United States, let alone Montana."

"Everything in that section is gone now. What else?"

She looked at him in surprise. "What do you mean?"

He swept his hand. "Imagine it gone. If you're taking this space on, and if you want it to disappear, assume it has happened. Anything else being kicked to the curb?"

"Nearly everything?"

Her voice was so soft he barely heard her words, but his heart leaped. "Perfect. What do you envision in its place?"

"What local artisans are there who might be interested in placing consignment pieces?"

"We tend to purchase outright unless artisans prefer consignment. Most don't."

"Oh. Okay."

"We carry pottery from Bayside Kiln in Jewel Lake. The potter, Trinity, goes to our church, actually. She bought back what didn't sell because she had a major order to fill for a gallery in Sunday Harbor." He pointed at one of the empty tables. "That's where we display her stuff. It sells pretty well."

"Good. Is there someone in the area who does stained glass? Any candle crafters? Candy makers?"

"I... I don't know." Maxwell pointed at the wide windows. "Stained glass would look nice with sunlight shining through, wouldn't it?"

Eryn nodded. "I was thinking a sweetgrass section with baskets and sachets and maybe candles. I'm sure there are other things that could be made from it and sold."

He narrowed his eyes and tried to think. "We can brainstorm that further. Anything else?"

She crossed to the books. "Montana history is great, but what about fiction? Coloring books? Books about gems — aren't they what Jewel Lake is named for?"

"Right. There have been all kinds mined in this area. Sapphires, rubies, agates, garnets — we're not far from the Garnet ghost town."

"Do you offer tours there?"

He blinked. "Um, no. Should we?" Offsite excursions would require a second activities director, as Paisley's docket was full enough.

"Why not? So, there should be a section for stuff to do

with gemstones. I'm not sure what would go in it because I don't know how they're discovered or mined or whatever."

"Fair enough." Maxwell nodded. "A sweetgrass section. A beefed-up book section. A gem section. More artisans. Anything else?"

She glanced his way, appearing hesitant.

"You look like you have an idea you're not sure I'll like. Anything and everything is on the figurative table today. Whatcha got? We can make it happen."

"I could… I could maybe come up with a simple quilt design for the ranch. Something for potholders or table runners."

He couldn't have stopped the smile spreading across his face even if he'd wanted to. "I would love to see that."

Eryn looked down at where her dressy shoe poked at the edge of a display unit. "Really?"

"Absolutely." Who had made this woman so unsure of herself? From the interactions Maxwell had observed, it wasn't her father. He might be a bit oblivious to the fact that Eryn's reactions weren't normal — weren't healthy — but he didn't seem to be adding to the burden.

Could it have been Amelia? Or being compared to her by everyone all the time? Because, while Maxwell could barely remember shy Eryn from childhood, Amelia stood out like a beacon, larger than life. She'd been confident. Forward. A bit brash, even.

What would it have been like to be her twin, always in her shadow?

"I'll show you later."

Maxwell pulled his focus back to Eryn. "You've been

drawing it already." It was written all over her face, even as she appeared reluctant to look at him.

"Yes? It's just a doodle. Not very good yet. Nothing firm."

He did his own share of doodling ideas for renovations. He'd be willing to bet her ideas were more polished than she was letting on.

"I've got a request for you."

This time, she did look at him and her shoulders braced. "What's that?"

"Can you put all that in writing? Maybe do some more research on local artisans and things like that, and make a written plan?"

"I... I could."

"Take a few weeks if you like." The last thing he wanted to do was make her feel pressured. Like her future depended on it. "Then I'd like to set up a meeting with Tate for you. Maybe at Thanksgiving when my grandfather is here as well, since he has a vested interest in all the areas of the guest ranch."

"That sounds nerve-wracking."

"I'll come with you if you like. And it's nothing to get anxious about. If that's the position you're applying to do, they'll be delighted with nearly anything you propose. It has to be an improvement over the slipshod way it's been run seasonally thus far, right?"

"Well..."

"You know I'm right." He chuckled. "I'll help with research if you want. Just point me in the right direction." Because wouldn't helping her with her proposal be a great excuse to spend time with her and get to know her without piling on pressure?

Yes. Yes, it would.

CHAPTER THIRTEEN

J uly 4, 2008

Small towns are dumb. The Independence Day parade was full of tractors pulling trailers with hokey farm stuff on them, like people dressed up as corn cobs. Ugh. If anyone from Wichita saw Gilead's parade they'd laugh until they peed their pants. And the fireworks lasted all of three minutes, tops. But Max and his brothers sat nearby with their mom, and I'm pretty sure he kept looking at me. I ACCIDEN-TALLY bumped into him when we were folding up our lawn chairs and he smiled at me and said hi. Oh my ~~gosh~~ (I'm not supposed to use that word) he has the cutest dimples. [three heart emojis]

Eryn grunted and slapped the diary closed. What did it matter that Amelia had noticed Maxwell's dimples? A girl would have to be blind not to.

Amelia wasn't here anymore. She was dead.

Eryn wasn't.

And why did that make her feel so guilty? It wasn't like

she'd driven the oncoming car or been anywhere in the vicinity. She'd never wished ill on her sister.

Gileadeans dabbed their eyes and spoke in hushed tones about a promising life cut short. But Eryn had felt relief — finally her sister would stop picking at her — and then guilt at the relief. Because death was final. Unless you were Jesus and could pop up again three days later — surprise! — and Amelia definitely wasn't God.

Neither was Eryn. She was not goodness and light and forgiveness and gentle harp music like the essence of some angelic being. She was bitter and angry and dark. Heavy metal music was a better representation.

She tucked the journal in the stack beneath her underwear in the rickety dresser drawer, fell back on the bed, and stared at the angled plank ceiling.

How could she still be so angry with her twin two years later? What caused that?

Eryn stifled a snort. *Everything* had caused it. Nothing she'd ever done had been as good as when Amelia did it. Eryn had had a slower start, in and out of hospitals a lot in the first couple of years, giving her sister a head start.

Amelia got better grades without even trying... but turned down her scholarship. Yeah, she said she hated small towns, but she'd hated hard work even more, and college would have required effort.

Amelia had snapped up every job she'd ever applied for but seemed bored after a while and drifted on to something else.

Eryn had started busing tables in high school and had worked her way up at the same diner until this move had forced her hand. Had her stick-to-it-iveness done her any good? Not likely.

Maxwell was giving her an opportunity to shift gears, not just locations. She didn't have any of the skills required for running a gift shop. She should just tell him no, that she was happy in the kitchen.

But she wasn't happy there... not that she knew for sure, since she wouldn't even start until tomorrow. However, the person who'd been in charge of the gift shop hadn't had the skills, either, by the looks of things. Eryn couldn't do worse.

Or... maybe she could. Maybe she'd put herself forward and then fall flat on her face with the entire staff of Sweet River Ranch watching.

With Maxwell watching.

Grr. Why did she care what he thought? He'd been on Amelia's radar, which should make him dead to Eryn, not by sister-code, but by default. She'd had so little that was hers alone, and here she was, a thousand miles and two years from her last interaction with her sister, and the only man who'd caught her attention had also caught Amelia's.

If her twin were here now, Maxwell would be flashing those dimples at Amelia, not Eryn. His opening line at the reunion had been sympathy for Amelia's passing, not, "Hey, how have you been, Eryn?"

Even here at the ranch, she wasn't free from Amelia. It was partly her own fault, though, since she kept reading her sister's old journals. She should start a bonfire and toss them in. Was there any point in rubbing salt in old wounds?

The sting reminded her that she was second best. Even

Dad kept saying things like, "Amelia would have loved it here."

No, she wouldn't. She hated farms. Hated smelly animals. Hated hicks.

But she'd had a crush on Maxwell Sullivan, so maybe she *would* have approved of the move.

"Eryn?" Dad called from the main floor. "I'm headed for bed now. I'll be up early to feed cattle with Joseph. Will you be okay?"

I'm 28 years old, Dad. It's not my first day of kindergarten. Of course, I'll be okay.

She forced a lilt into her voice. "Have fun! I'm working from nine to one. Maybe I'll see you in the dining hall at lunch."

"I think you'll like working for Nadine. She seems nice."

Eryn rolled her eyes, thankful Dad couldn't see. "Yes, she does. See you tomorrow, Dad."

"Good night." His bedroom door closed.

She should turn out her light and try to sleep, too, but her brain was bouncing all over the place. Her gaze brushed over her Bible on the nightstand. She hadn't been reading regularly since before the reunion.

Eryn winced. Since *way* before the reunion.

God felt so distant.

What was the saying? That God hadn't moved. She had. If she turned around, He'd be right there, close by, like He'd always been. But… had He ever truly been there?

She could scarcely have grown up in Gilead and attended the Bible college's passion play every year since childhood without recognizing and accepting Jesus' sacrifice on her behalf.

Eryn believed it. She did. But God still felt distant.

She picked up her Bible and paged through it. Where had she even been reading when she'd trailed off last time? Ugh. It had been *that* long.

Psalms were good. Hadn't David been harassed and chased and belittled before he became king? There was a lot of lamenting in those poems, if Eryn remembered correctly. She flipped through that section, her eye catching on Psalm 139.

You have searched me, Lord, and you know me. You know when I sit and when I rise; you perceive my thoughts from afar. You discern my going out and my lying down; you are familiar with all my ways. Before a word is on my tongue you, Lord, know it completely.

The psalm went on, but Eryn's attention had been snagged by the opening lines. If God truly perceived her thoughts, then He knew how she struggled with the memories of a lifetime of being Amelia's twin. He was familiar with *all* her ways.

And, by implication, loved her anyway.

Oh, Dad loved her for who she was. Mom had, too, though it had seemed like Amelia was her favorite. But Amelia had always resented Eryn in her life. Resented sharing everything, especially birthdays.

You have searched me, Lord, and you know me.

This didn't feel as comforting as it should. Because knowing Eryn was the first step to understanding how unworthy she was. Best to keep Maxwell in the dark about that for as long as possible.

AROUND HIM, Maxwell's crew jumped into the current project, rejuvenated by their two-week break. Jordan and Tory painted one of the loft bedrooms, Jordan cutting in along the ceiling with a steady hand, and his helper following with a roller.

In the kitchen, Steve installed backsplash tile while Janessa inspected the evenness of the grout lines. Steve glowered at her and said she was making him nervous.

Maxwell checked his watch. Why wasn't it noon yet? Not that he was all that hungry, but that was when he'd see Eryn again. How was her morning going with Aunt Nadine? It would be fine.

Finally, he called time, and Tory immediately hollered down the stairs with, "We need ten more minutes. Meet you there."

Steve flexed his shoulder muscles in the kitchen. "Nearly done. Just need to clean the tools. Unless Janessa wants to do it."

"As if."

Maxwell should wait for his crew... but why? He jingled his truck fob in his pocket. "I've got something to check on. See you there." The something was Eryn, but he didn't need to tell them that.

A few minutes later he strode into the dining hall to find Tate and Graham at a table with an open laptop between them. "Hey, guys."

Tate glanced up, a smile creasing his face. "Hey. How's things on Ladybug Lane?"

Maxwell chuckled, forcing himself to focus on his brother rather than glancing beyond the counter into the kitchen. "You'll never believe the ladybug tiles Janessa found. We're using them as accents in a couple of the bathrooms."

"Too funny."

Graham frowned. "I saw the invoice for those."

Maxwell managed not to roll his eyes. This was a perfect example of why he preferred flipping houses on his own, not answerable to Sullivan Enterprises. "They were a minor expense that will bring plenty of smiles."

"Right."

They did need Graham — or someone like him — as CFO. Expenses could get way out of hand rehabbing this ranch, not that Grandfather's pockets weren't plenty deep enough to handle it all.

Maxwell glanced toward the kitchen. "Lunch smells good."

"You're here early." Tate's eyebrows tilted up. "The bell won't ring for another five minutes."

"I was in the vicinity." At least, after he'd driven down from Ladybug, he had been. He scanned the whiteboard. "Split pea soup and biscuits. Mmm, sounds good."

"You don't have to pretend, you know." Tate's voice was laced with humor.

"Pretend what?"

"That I don't know why you're here early, the guy who nearly always charges in just before the line closes."

"What am I missing?" Graham's gaze shifted back and forth between them.

Tate leaned toward Graham, his eyes still on Maxwell standing beside the table. "You've been busy, what with the honeymoon and all."

Graham's neck and face flamed red in half a second flat.

"But while you were gone, Maxwell hired us a new farm manager and kitchen help for Aunt Nadine. I know you saw the payroll paperwork."

"Yes?"

"My little brother is smitten."

Thankfully, Tate's voice had lowered into a conspiratorial tone, because the women in the kitchen weren't that far away.

Eryn looked adorable even with her blond hair wrapped in a braid around her head and a plaid apron over her jeans and green staff T-shirt. She didn't seem to have overheard Tate... or even noticed Maxwell's entry, for that matter.

He squelched the slight feeling of disappointment.

"Smitten?" Graham looked between Maxwell and Eryn. "Oh!"

"Yeah, he's following in our footsteps, yours and mine," Tate continued, still smirking. "Hiring our girls here to keep them nearby while they're being wooed."

"That's not how it was with Cadence!" Graham protested.

Tate tilted an eyebrow up and studied their cousin.

"Okay, a little bit. But I didn't think I stood a chance."

It had been entertaining to watch shy, geeky Graham fall in love over the summer, just as fun as it had been to observe Tate and Stephanie's romantic drama play out earlier in the spring.

Great. Everyone had a front-row seat to Maxwell's pursuit of Eryn. He might as well hand out bags of popcorn now.

It didn't really bother him so much. He was used to his

family and how they had each other's back by being *in* each other's faces. Even Bryce did, for all his disparaging talk. If Bryce really didn't want to toe the family line, he could put his business degree to use elsewhere. Yeah, he'd barely squeaked through college — he'd been too busy partying to take studying seriously — but he'd graduated. He kept working for Grandfather because it was easier than hustling out in the real world. He made more money for less work.

Maxwell hadn't bothered with post-secondary schooling, though he'd started taking online courses before moving to Montana. Seemed a guy who ran his own business should have a bit more education than the school of hard knocks.

"See how she keeps looking over here?" Tate stage whispered. "She wasn't doing that before my kid brother came in, but now she can't stop."

Maxwell's gaze slipped to see Eryn focusing on plating a batch of biscuits. She didn't seem aware of him at all.

Graham snickered. "You mean, like he keeps looking at her?"

Busted. Was there any point in denying it?

Maxwell pulled out a chair, turned it, and straddled it where he could still see into the kitchen. "I've got news for you two."

"Oh?" Tate drawled, leaning back. "You're a faster mover than I gave you credit for."

"Not that, dingbat." Maxwell shoved his brother's shoulder. "She's really shy. Could you two not make a production out of this and scare her off before I even have a chance?"

"Shy, hmm?" Tate's eyes danced.

"She seems insecure," Graham affirmed. "I know what that's like."

At least one of these doofuses took Maxwell seriously. Cadence had been really good for Graham, though she'd been plenty insecure herself when she'd bolted to the ranch last year after being jilted days before her wedding. Graham had done the bravest, most impulsive thing he'd ever done by helping her run away and giving her a safe place to land.

There were more similarities than Maxwell had realized.

Tate leaned in. "I think you should just declare yourself to her."

Hadn't he already done that? And she was interested, but he needed to go easy. She was timid, skittish like a yearling filly.

Hmm. Now there was a thought. Nutmeg's yearling filly, Echo, didn't trust easily. Would Eryn be drawn to the young horse? How about vice versa?

It was worth talking to Weston about.

CHAPTER FOURTEEN

Thanks for your help today." Nadine Kline turned from where she loaded the dishwasher with a smile on her face.

Eryn shifted from one foot to the other. "I shouldn't leave while there's still work to be done." Also, she couldn't believe Nadine had been doing this alone half the time.

Nadine laughed. "It's never done, so don't worry about it. You made the soup for lunch and prepped half of dinner plus made dessert. That apple cake smells amazing, by the way. I hope you have more recipes like that up your sleeve."

Whew. "Thank you. I like to bake, so I'll be happy to do more. And there are lots of apples."

"I was thinking of pie with a sourdough crust."

"I've never worked with sourdough. Never baked bread of any kind. Yours is delicious."

"I can teach you." Nadine poked her chin toward the warming oven near the industrial-size range. "Tomorrow's dough is already fermenting."

"I'd love to learn." It was true. Even though Eryn didn't

love cooking, baking was something else. "Tell me when to be here."

"There's time enough for that next week." Nadine's gaze slipped past Eryn, and she smiled. "Hey, Maxwell."

"Hi, Aunt Nadine."

Eryn couldn't keep from turning. Ack! How had she not heard him sneak up right behind her? She pressed her hand over her heart. "You startled me!"

"Sorry." The grin revealed a dimple that did not look the tiniest bit repentant. "I heard you were off at one, and I was hoping you'd come to the stable with me."

Eryn fingered the hem of her apron. "I'm not dressed for riding."

Maxwell's warm gaze slid to her toes and back to her face. "You look great to me, though you might want to leave the apron."

Nadine coughed and turned away, waving her hand. "Don't mind me."

"There's someone over there I want you to meet. Did you walk down this morning or drive? I've got one of the golf carts, so I'm happy to take you by Hummingbird Lane if you want to change before we go to the stable. Not that you need to."

"Who do you want me to meet?" Eryn untied her apron and slipped the loop over her head. Whether she went with Maxwell or not, her shift was done.

"It's a surprise." He grinned.

That guy. Did he have any idea the power in those dimples? Eryn doubted it, or he wouldn't flash them so regularly.

"Come on. You know you want to, right? Unless…" He studied her. "Unless you're tired and need a break."

Was he kidding her right now? She was an introvert and could always use a break from people if she'd spent five minutes with them, let alone four hours. On the other hand, this was Maxwell, and he didn't add that sort of stress. He'd become a safe landing place, and the stable sounded quiet and welcoming.

She lifted her chin. "I'll come, but I would like to change first, please."

Was that relief on his face? Did he really think she had the capacity to turn him down?

A few minutes later, they pulled in front of the stable where Weston was working a young horse on a longe line. Since Maxwell stayed sitting on the cart, watching, Eryn did, too.

After a moment she asked, "What is he doing?"

"That's Echo, Nutmeg's two-year-old. She's… skittish."

Eryn watched for clues. The filly's eyes grew wide when Weston, murmuring softly, stepped closer, his hand outstretched with something on it. Echo seemed more fearful than curious as she backed away, nostrils flaring. "Is that normal behavior?"

Maxwell shrugged but shook his head slightly. "Not from what Weston told me. He picked Nutmeg and Echo up at an auction last spring. The mare settled in pretty well, but Echo? He hasn't been able to win her trust."

Eryn studied the head wrangler and how he worked with the young horse. "He's patient."

"He is." Maxwell chuckled softly. "Way more than I could ever be. At least two-by-fours and tiles and cans of paint can't get it in their heads that they don't want to do what you bought them for."

"I hadn't thought of that. I've always worked with people. My boss at Debby's was demanding, and the other workers and the diners weren't always kind. It wears on a person."

Maxwell gestured to Weston. "You should have seen my cousin back at the beginning. He's quiet and gruff now, but he was downright angry all the time then... except with the horses. He's always had all the patience in the world with them. People? Not so much."

Eryn was beginning to think she should have been in a different line of work all along. Maybe the gift shop would be a good fit for that. Less peopley, at least in the offseason. But there wasn't really any solo job at Sweet River, except maybe Dad's.

"You seem to like being around people, though." At least, he worked with a crew, and he wouldn't be in that sort of business if he hated them. Right?

"Some of them." The lines around Maxwell's eyes crinkled when he smiled. "If they want to hustle and work as a team, we get along great. If they're too independent or too lazy — if they don't seem able to follow orders or own their mistakes — they usually don't last too long working for me."

Was there a warning in that? Eryn wasn't sure if she had that kind of independent streak or not. She'd never pushed the limits but gone along with expectations. Amelia had prodded enough for them both, and maybe Eryn had simply tried to form a counterbalance.

Maybe, just maybe, she'd done herself a disservice by

not rocking the boat and figuring out who she really was and what she wanted to do with her life. Amelia had spent her whole life trying to prove she wasn't the same as Eryn. Eryn had spent her life trying to prove she was a nice person, even if her sister wasn't.

Had she needed to show that to anyone? Maybe she could have lived it out by being herself.

Maxwell rose and stretched his hand to her. "Come on. I want you to meet Echo."

ERYN's startled gaze met his. "You brought me here to meet a horse?"

"I did." He grinned. "Is that okay?"

"Sure. I guess." She stood and accepted his hand as she jumped off the cart.

Made him feel like a hero from an old western helping a genteel lady off a stagecoach. Maxwell scoffed lightly under his breath. *Wrong millennium, Sullivan.*

She was no pampered debutante. She was far, far more self-sufficient. Thank the Lord for all the changes in women's rights since those old days. The women on his crew did all the same jobs the guys did.

Eryn let go of his grip, approached the corral slowly, and leaned her arms on the top rail, watching Echo.

Maxwell's hand felt empty without hers in it. He followed her and mimicked her stance, his shoulder pressed against hers. "What do you think of her?"

"I'm not sure why it matters?"

He hesitated, searching her face. "There are dozens of

other horses, so Weston and Darrell don't have all the time Echo needs."

Her gaze narrowed. "And you think I have time? I know nothing about horses!"

Had Maxwell misjudged her? "You have more time than they have, but if you aren't interested in hanging out with her, you certainly don't have to." He shifted so he wasn't touching her and forced his gaze back to the filly.

Weston glanced toward the visitors, eyebrows raised. He had Echo circling on the longe line, more slowly now.

How to answer the unspoken question? But Maxwell wouldn't give up on Eryn so easily. He'd probably bungled the question. He gave a slight nod to his cousin.

Weston waited for Echo to slow to a walk and complete the circuit a couple of more times as he slowly shortened the line, reeling the filly closer and closer until he hooked his fingers on the halter strap. Echo pulled back, eyes wide, and Weston spoke soothingly to her, too quietly for Maxwell to pick out more than the tone.

"We think she was mistreated at the other place. Or maybe only neglected, as if that's not bad enough." Maxwell kept his voice similarly low as Weston brought Echo closer to the rail.

"She's beautiful," Eryn whispered.

Maxwell managed a complete breath. "She is." He stopped before adding that Eryn was, too. No, today's step was about winning Echo's trust.

"Are there apple pieces?"

Maxwell nodded to the bucket hung over a fence post nearby. "You want to feed her? You can get inside the pen, if you like. Just—"

"Just move slowly and don't startle her. Got it."

"Yeah."

Effortlessly, Eryn swung over the corral like the experienced farm girl she was. The Ralstons might not have had horses in many years, but she certainly knew animals, all the same. She scooped her hand into the apple bucket then held it out toward the filly. "Who's a pretty girl? Echo, that's who. Hey, Echo, want to be friends?"

Weston met Maxwell's gaze over the filly's back. His nod was miniscule, but Maxwell cheered inside at his cousin's approval.

Echo stretched toward Eryn then pulled back. Weston murmured something to the filly.

Sounded like the way Stephanie talked to baby Simon, honestly. The tone of voice, the soothing words, the focus on stillness. And was Maxwell holding his breath, awaiting the outcome? Sure was. He managed a breath or two as he focused on the tableau in front of him.

Weston kept murmuring sweet nothings to Echo, and Eryn said them back. If Maxwell wasn't so certain of Weston's adoration of his fiancée, Paisley, he'd have been a little jealous of the way they tag-teamed that filly like they'd been doing it their entire lives.

After a few minutes of the shy dance, Echo nipped a piece of apple from Eryn's palm. By the third morsel, she allowed Eryn to touch the side of her muzzle.

"Aren't you soft? Do you like that?"

Maxwell strained to hear her voice, his heart welling at the picture the woman and the horse made together. Once again, his gaze met Weston's. This time, the wrangler's approving nod was firmer.

Weston continued in the same sing-song voice he'd been using on Echo. "She likes you. Would you be interested in hanging around with her for a bit most afternoons? You can bring your laptop if you have stuff to do. We've got access to the resort Wi-Fi here."

Eryn's head snapped up, and Echo shied back, but Weston still held the halter.

"Sorry. I thought Maxwell mentioned that to you?"

"Not precisely." Eryn shot Maxwell an accusatory glance. "He just mentioned he had someone he wanted me to meet. Someone who needed time and attention."

"Right?" Weston sounded confused.

One more thing Maxwell had in common with his cousin. "If you're working on the gift shop proposal, you could do that from here, if you wanted."

"From where, exactly? It's October, and it's not going to get warmer over the next few weeks."

"Oh! We've got a place inside we can set up for you. A space big enough for Echo to hang out nearby." Weston thumbed toward the stable. "Want to see? But also, if you don't want to — if you don't have time — it's okay. She'll survive."

"Survive?" Eryn looked between him and the filly a couple of times. "Show me."

Maxwell resisted the urge to pump his fist. She might not know it yet, but she'd already agreed.

Weston ushered Eryn in front of him as he led Echo into the stable.

No way was Maxwell being left out of this. He entered via the main doors and waited for a few seconds for his eyes to adjust before following his ears toward Echo's box stall.

"See, we've got her in this one by the office, because she needs all the extra attention we can give her." Weston rubbed his jaw. "Thing is, neither Darrell nor I sit around in there. We're too busy for that kind of nonsense."

Eryn stiffened.

Bad wording, cousin.

"But if your job is already on a computer — Max said you had a research project — then maybe it would work for you?"

Calling the nook an office was a bit of a stretch. If Grandfather had noticed what the facilities were like, he'd have insisted on building a proper, enclosed room where not just anyone could wander into the area.

"I'll just clear space." Weston gathered up dusty files and stacked them off to one side. "I can requisition a better chair, too. It's just that Darrell or I rarely sit here for more than five minutes. Not if we can help it."

Eryn cast a questioning glance at Maxwell. "We could try it for a few days. I'm working mornings in the kitchen. I might not be super regular here."

"I'd be grateful if you'd try. She's a good temperament. Has good lines. But she has trust issues."

Maxwell held his breath. Would Eryn feel too set up? But it wasn't like they'd looked for a needy filly to create a project for her. Echo had been here for several months already.

"What would I need to do?"

"They say a person shouldn't sit at the computer all the time without taking breaks." Weston clearly didn't understand how anyone could do that, anyway. "So, get up, stretch, talk to Echo, feed her an apple chunk or a carrot, touch her face, maybe brush her a little, and go back to what you were doing. Maxwell mentioned you're interested in turning that poor excuse for a gift shop around?"

"Maybe." She sent Maxwell a glare.

Oops. Maybe he'd been telling tales out of turn. But either way, if she and Echo could help each other, wouldn't that be a win all the way around?

CHAPTER FIFTEEN

axwell?"

His name sounded sweet on Eryn's lips, even if she asked it tentatively. "Yes?"

"I was wondering…" She twisted her hands together.

He waited, holding his smile in place. It took a moment.

"I want to talk to some of the artisans in Jewel Lake, but I'm not sure."

"Certain about what?" he asked, when the silence had lingered too long.

"I don't have the authority to speak on behalf of the ranch. Or of the gift shop."

"You're asking them questions about availability, right? Gathering information?"

"Right, but…"

Light trickled in. "Would you like me to come with you?"

She nodded, biting her lip and barely meeting his gaze. "I know you're super busy, though."

"My crew doesn't need me hovering every minute. I

could take a day off. How about Monday? You might want to call ahead and set up appointments. Not everyone has gallery hours in October."

"I can do that, but it's only a half day, since I work in the kitchen in the morning."

"Ask Nadine for the entire day off. That would give us time to meet more artisans."

"I shouldn't ask."

"I can, if you won't. She'll be happy to let you go, you know." Especially if she suspected something was brewing between them. "Your pay won't be docked for time off."

Eryn blinked. "But it should be."

"It's all ranch business."

"But…" She shook her head. "This is all new to me. I know I've been here over a week, but it's so different."

"I get that." Working for Grandfather again after eight years on his own had been quite an adjustment for Maxwell, as well. He could see how Eryn might not be sure of her place. "You're doing great with Echo, by the way."

Eryn's cheeks pinked. "She's wonderful."

"She follows you around like a puppy." Maxwell chuckled. "But that's not today's topic, sorry. Will you ask Nadine, or shall I? Because I'd like to take you for lunch in town between appointments. And…" Was she ready? Only one way to find out. "And dinner. Maybe a movie, depending on what's playing."

Her gaze flew to meet his. "Like a…?"

"Not just *like* a date, but actually a date."

"Oh."

Not a resounding response, but better than he'd expected. "I meant what I've said before. I want to get to know you better, and I think — I hope — you might be a tiny bit interested in that, too?"

"Maybe?"

Maxwell touched her arm. "I'm not sure what I've done to make you so hesitant, but I'll take the maybe. Because I'm in."

"I thought you'd probably forgotten all that by now."

He let his fingers trail down to her hand before tangling them with hers. "Not a chance. I just didn't want to scare you and make you shy away."

A tiny smile poked at her lips. "Like Echo."

"Sort of like her, yes. But far more important than any horse could ever be."

"Don't let Weston hear you say that."

Maxwell chuckled. "Pre-Paisley, you'd be right, but I think he's come around to realizing human relationships supersede equine. At least one human relationship."

"He and Paisley are cute. They're so different from each other."

"They really are. I don't know if she told you, but she chased Weston down for well over a year before she caught him."

"She told me."

Maxwell laughed. "Of course, she did. Paisley has no trouble talking to anyone about anything. If I didn't want to spend time with you so much, I'd suggest that you take her to Jewel Lake to visit artisans. She'd love it."

"She would." Eryn's eyes searched his.

Her fingers were still twined with his. He squeezed a little. "I'm not giving her the chance. Not this time."

"Okay." Eryn straightened and tugged her hand free of his. "I'll ask Nadine and get back to you."

"Sure. You can catch me at mealtime, or you've got my number." Not that she'd used it since arriving at the ranch. "I look forward to spending the day with you."

"Thanks. Do you know if my dad is doing okay at his job? Weston says he's fine when I ask."

"Then he's fine. Are you worried about him?"

"All of this…" Eryn's gesture seemed to take in all of Sweet River. "It still seems like a dream sometimes. Like I'll wake up and find myself in my old bed back in Gilead. Only, that was going to end, either way."

"It's not a dream. Or, if it is, I'm in it with you, and thankful to be there."

"That's good." But she sounded tentative.

"No one's going to take this opportunity away from you and your father, Eryn. You're here, secure, until or unless you choose to go elsewhere." He waited until her gaze met his. "And I'm hoping and praying that never happens."

"Amelia…"

Why did she keep bringing up her twin's name? Maxwell didn't care about Amelia. They'd only been kids when they'd had their brief moment. It hadn't lasted long and certainly hadn't been deep. What 13-year-olds knew anything about real love, anyway? Not a single one.

I love you, Maxwell.

Yeah, well, he hadn't said it back. Not like she wanted. He'd never said those words to anyone besides his mother. His relationship with Dad certainly wasn't based on inter-changes like that. A thump on the back and a thumbs-up was as affirmative and mushy as Dad got. As for his brothers? Ha! Not a chance.

"Amelia thought you were pretty cool."

Maxwell blinked himself back into the moment as his mind raced, discarding several responses as quickly as they flitted through. He posed in a weightlifter's muscular stance. "I *was* pretty cool. For a scrawny kid."

As he'd hoped, Eryn grinned at that. "Yeah, you were."

Wait, what? "You noticed me back then?"

The pink tinge returned to her cheeks. "It was hard not to."

"Huh. I never knew."

"Because you barely knew I existed. It's okay. I was used to it."

He studied her face. "Your sister was a force to be reckoned with." And there was more going on than he'd realized. Maybe having a twin hadn't been all he'd assumed.

"She was. I, um, should get going. Echo is probably wondering where I am." Eryn turned away.

Maxwell caught her arm. "Eryn? As you know, I hadn't seen Amelia since high school. But you have depth that she never had, unless she acquired it later."

Eryn looked at where his hand rested beside her elbow. "Amelia didn't do deep."

His hunch appeared to be correct. He wouldn't push now, but he'd keep watching for the clues he'd likely missed earlier about the twins' relationship. It seemed it hadn't been sunshine-and-roses. Maybe Amelia was responsible for Eryn's hesitant nature. That seemed to fit, but he couldn't be sure.

"She might not have matured, but I guess that's neither

here nor there anymore. I'm sorry — it seems she died without having grown beyond that."

Eryn's nod was more like a sharp jerk of her head.

There was definitely more to the story than he'd ferreted out yet, but he had time. He might be quick and decisive in his renovation business, but he could be patient.

He could at least try to be.

MAKING cold calls was exquisitely painful, but Eryn took a deep breath and punched in the first number. She'd picked the potter, because the woman had already sold her work at the ranch, and Maxwell said she went to the same church.

"You've reached Trinity Kennedy at Bayside Kiln. How may I help you?"

"Hi, I'm Eryn Ralston, calling from Sweet River Ranch." She took a deep breath and read the script she'd prepared. "I'm creating a business plan for the gift shop here. I know you've sold some of your pottery here in the past few years, but there isn't any onsite now, and I'd like to see your line and talk to you about it, if you have time? I'll be in town on Monday."

"Monday…"

Eryn heard some tapping.

"Monday at four should work, if that's all right? My studio is in Agate Bay."

Good thing Maxwell would be driving. He'd know how to find that, right? Because Eryn had no clue, and her car was too ancient for GPS. "That sounds great. I can't wait to meet you on Monday."

"Same! See you then. Also, I'm glad to hear someone is taking on that gift shop. It needs it."

Eryn agreed, tapped to end the call, and took a few deep breaths. That hadn't gone too badly, but then, Trinity hadn't precisely been a cold call. Cold for Eryn, but not for the ranch.

Echo nickered and nudged Eryn's shoulder.

Eryn turned and wrapped her arms around the filly's neck. "Hey, how did you know I needed a friend?"

An equine sigh misted down Eryn's back.

"Not talking about it, huh?" She laughed, feeling some of the tension dissipate. Had Maxwell realized how therapeutic hanging around Echo would be for Eryn? She'd thought it was for the filly's sake, but she was beginning to wonder if he'd been more perceptive than she'd given him credit for.

Should she be offended that he thought hanging around a horse would be helpful to her? Hmm.

But then Weston often rode out surly and returned at peace. Several of the other staff members had come through the stables the past few days, and Eryn had noticed the same thing from them. Maybe not grumpy like Weston, but tense… and then soothed and smiling upon their return, whether it was twenty minutes or two hours later.

So… if that's what he'd been thinking for her, she couldn't be annoyed. It seemed a time-tested technique. She should get Dad riding, but he was keeping pretty busy with Joseph preparing the cattle for the upcoming winter. Still, didn't Dad need a break, too?

Eryn patted Echo's mane one more time and turned back to the makeshift office. Next up: Aurora Glassworks. Hopefully this artisan would be as nice as Trinity had been.

And then there were five more, including an indigenous woman up near Saint Ignatius who created items from sweetgrass. That might be farther than Maxwell would want to drive on Monday, though. But maybe she should call the woman first and see if they could come in the morning? That would leave the afternoon clear for Jewel Lake artisans.

Eryn reshuffled her notes and tapped in Kaya's phone number.

The woman seemed hesitant at first but warmed to the idea of meeting Eryn and considering placing some of her products in the gift shop, so long as she could maintain creative control of her display.

Eryn gladly agreed as they set up a meeting time. Then she jumped to her feet and shook out her hands before approaching Echo with a curry brush. A few minutes grooming the filly would settle her enough to make another phone call or two.

Yeah, Maxwell had known what he was doing, pairing them together.

Voices came from the corral, and Eryn glanced toward the open doors as Weston and Darrell entered, leading two horses.

"Hey, Eryn." Weston almost managed to smile. "How's our favorite girl today?"

There was absolutely no doubt he meant Echo. "She's good."

Weston circled the horse, running his hands over her back and withers, before meeting Eryn's gaze again. "Want to longe her?"

"Longe?" Did he mean…?

"Run her in easy circles for exercise like we did the other day when you were here."

"Me?"

"Sure. Why not? There's not much to it. It just takes a little time and attention."

Maybe she'd find herself on the stable's payroll. The thought was a little enticing, honestly. But, as Maxwell had commented, the employee was the same, regardless of which part of the resort she worked. No doubt, the areas that required specialized knowledge paid better, though. She wouldn't qualify as a stable hand under those stipulations.

She cast a glance at her phone list. They could wait an hour, right? "Sure. I'd like to learn to do that with Echo."

Weston tipped his head toward the doors. "Bring her along, then. Meet you in the round pen."

"Come on, Echo. Want some exercise? I bet you'd rather run up the trails than in circles, though."

Wouldn't anyone?

CHAPTER SIXTEEN

L ook at you! You won Kaya over just like that."
Maxwell handed Eryn back into his pickup truck.
"And it's only 10 a.m."

Eryn grinned as she buckled up, wiggling in her seat in a sort of dance. "She's so nice, and her products are amazing."

Maxwell managed to dispel the impulse to lean in and kiss her, right then and there. It wasn't the time or place, but soon. Maybe even today. He backed away, closed the door, and rounded the truck.

A minute later, they were headed south again. He glanced across the cab and couldn't help but smile back at the delight still on Eryn's face. Not that he wanted to pull a Westonish frown. "How do you feel about that gift shop now?"

Her eyes shone. "I can see it all in my imagination already. Do you think it might actually happen?"

"Of course. Why wouldn't it?"

"It's not like I know what I'm doing."

"I beg to differ." Maxwell reached across and covered her hand with his.

She stared at it for a moment before turning hers to twine her fingers around his.

Success! "You've got vision, which is more than our previous manager had."

"Am I taking someone else's job?" Eryn frowned.

Maxwell tried to remember who had even run the shop last year. Failed, but then, he hadn't hung around the lodge much. He and his crew had been working flat out on Firefly Lane back then, where the previous owners had begun renovations before running out of money, leaving the cottages uninhabitable.

"Tate just won't post that position with the others when he hires for next summer. The previous manager was probably a college student who might not even reapply. Because we have mostly seasonal work, we get a lot of students. A lot of staff turnover."

"That makes sense."

He squeezed her fingers gently. "Don't worry about it. That person obviously wasn't suited to the position. You are, and it will flourish."

"Do you really think so?"

"I know so."

"You can't possibly be as certain as you sound."

"Why not? I've been watching you." He laughed. "That sounds creepy. But I've seen how excited this makes you, I've seen your hard work. I know making all those calls wasn't easy for you, but you did it, and the artisans are happy to meet with you. I'd say you're well on your way with that kiosk of Kaya's. I love the idea of using the half-canoe as a display for her traditional pieces. It will get a lot of attention. Where in the store are you thinking?"

"Didn't I show you the sketch I made of the room? It will need adjusting as I get confirmation from artisans and see how much space each will need. Like the half-canoe can't be in the middle, since it's so tall. I was thinking beside the entry-hall window."

"Hmm. That could work." Maxwell nodded. "And no, I didn't see a sketch. I can't wait to, though." Then he could mock it up on his CAD program. That would be fun. "The candy maker is next, right? She's in Missoula?"

Eryn nodded. "And then the stained-glass artist at 1:00 in Jewel Lake, the jeweler at 2:00, the leather crafter at 3:00, and the potter at 4:00. There's also a blacksmith who fashions wrought-iron pieces, but his voicemail says he's away in October. I'll have to follow up with him later."

"Wow. I can see it all already. What a cool showcase of local talent." Maxwell merged onto I-90 eastbound. "Have you had a chance to work on the quilt design?"

She wrinkled her nose. "It won't be half as impressive as all that other stuff, so I probably won't bother."

"Hey. Don't shortchange yourself."

"I'm not. I know I'm not that good."

"Not that you've let me see any of your work to judge for myself."

"It's all packed away. I doubt I'll open any of it until we move into the farmhouse next month."

"I get that." He did. But it seemed like she was stalling, her lack of confidence in herself roaring to the forefront again. Should he push her? Maybe not today. She was putting herself out there on behalf of the gift shop — on behalf of Sweet River Ranch — and that was likely usurping all the peopling capacity she had for right now.

Maxwell might not be an introvert, but he'd done some reading to try to understand how those like Graham and Weston and Jude functioned. It was a mystery to someone who thrived on the buzz of people and action, but hey, God hadn't created only one sort of personality. How boring would that be?

Though he'd never expected to be this drawn to someone his polar opposite. Eryn had so many layers that it could be a lifelong project to understand what made her tick. Most everything Maxwell tackled was in bite-sized pieces where he could check details off his to-do list every single day. Progress could be charted. *Was* charted, so that the members of his team could see at a glance the status of each of the cottages on Ladybug Lane. His crew was staggered through several at a time, with utilities being worked on in one, cabinetry in another, painting and tiling in a third, and flooring in another. Thankfully, the vinyl planks had finally shown up Friday, so Jordan and Tory were installing them this week in #4.

"…candy maker."

Maxwell gave his head a shake. "Sorry. I was plotting my own crew's work week. What about the candy maker?" He couldn't believe his mind had drifted to work while he was out with Eryn. How pathetic was that?

"Nothing, I was just thinking out loud."

"I want to hear."

She shook her head and turned to look out the window.

Drat. If only he could barricade his brain. "What kind of candy are we talking? Fudge? Peanut brittle?"

"Hard candies. Maybe tourists won't like them anyway."

"People like anything sweet." Maxwell liked sweet Eryn, and he should stop hurting her by ignoring her while they were together. But he couldn't talk all the time, and she wasn't given to a lot of chatter. Where else was his brain supposed to go besides work? Eight years of flipping houses had honed his focus.

"There's a candy place in Helena, too, I found in search. It's called Parrot Confectionary. I wonder if they sell wholesale?"

"Helena?" That was an hour and a half in the opposite direction and not compatible with today's outing. "We could check it out sometime. It's the State Capitol and worth the visit from what I hear. The architecture is off the charts."

Eryn chuckled. "I want to eat candy, and you're thinking of buildings?"

"Helena was the wealthiest city in the world per capita in the 1880s when it became Montana's capital. I've seen photos of the mansion district. Super impressive houses."

"Fancier than your mom's house in Gilead?"

Maxwell blinked and glanced over at Eryn. "Yes? The house in Gilead is fairly ordinary, all things considered." Too late, he remembered the state of the Ralston farmhouse a mere few miles away. "At least, it didn't seem special to me, growing up. It was just where we lived."

And Eryn's pensive face closed off.

WHAT WAS SHE THINKING, harboring romantic fantasies about Maxwell Sullivan? If the house in Gilead was nothing special, he'd forgotten how the other 99.9% of America lived. More likely, he'd never known. Never thought about it.

Inexplicably, he was fascinated by her right now, but that wouldn't last. He'd remember her lowly circumstances and how her dad had lost the farm. It might be fun for him to be a hero right now — and she couldn't deny that he'd made a huge difference in her life, hers and Dad's — but the novelty would wear off. When it came time for him to settle down, it would be with a woman who didn't gape at the opulence of his family home.

She didn't stand a chance, nor should she. Getting out of Kansas was good, though. Dad seemed to love what he was doing on the ranch. Eryn would do her best to put the gift shop on a firm footing, then she'd be better off looking for a different job nearby where she could still see Dad often. Maybe she could serve at the Golden Grill or somewhere like that.

Anyplace where she wouldn't run into Maxwell several times a day and wonder when he'd tire of her, because it was coming. The second shoe always landed on the floor, sooner or later.

But the next few hours flew by as they chatted with assorted artisans, ending up in a lovely lakeside pottery studio in a former carriage house.

"This is lovely," Eryn breathed, looking around. The space was tidier than that of any other artisan she'd met today.

"I'm glad you like it." The potter, Trinity, smiled, her

gaze not quite meeting Eryn's, though the words sounded genuine enough.

"Which pieces have sold best at our gift shop in the past?" Eryn pulled out her tablet to take notes.

"Tourists seem to love mugs," Trinity replied. "We've also done well with small platters. Things that can go in a carry-on without too much chance of breakage."

"That makes sense." Stained glass might not be the best option, in that case, though Aurora had seemed quite interested in displaying suncatchers of assorted styles.

"Are these all the styles you're currently producing?" The mossy greens were lovely, but Eryn had been envisioning something in blue or gray.

"Yes. I'm not into experimenting quite as much as I used to do."

"Oh? Why's that?" Most artisans seemed to want to stretch, not pull back.

The woman smiled. "I'm 80% blind, and my husband has his own business, so he isn't always here to bounce ideas off of or tell me if something works."

"Blind?" It might have seemed insensitive to blurt the word back to the potter, but it would explain the lack of solid eye contact. "You can do all this without actually seeing it?"

Mind blown.

"I have some peripheral vision, but that's not helpful for detailing."

Maxwell shifted beside Eryn. "This is amazing work, Trinity. I was super impressed even before you told us that."

"Yes, I agree." Eryn sidled closer to Maxwell, not that blindness was contagious.

"I have a form of macular dystrophy called Best Disease. It only began manifesting about five or six years ago. Thankfully, I already knew my way around my studio before then, but there are stories of potters who started after blindness occurred, and some who never had sight to begin with. At least, I remember what colors are and how they work together. Also, Dale helps a lot with that when he's home."

"Amazing," Eryn breathed. The pieces were truly breathtaking on their own. Now they seemed even more special. "Your website didn't say anything about it."

Trinity shrugged and laughed. "I don't want pity purchases. I want people to buy my pieces because they connect with them. I don't sell retail from the studio, so I rarely meet the final owners. In my early days, I relied on craft fairs and the like, but I'm grateful I was well enough established when I moved back to Jewel Lake to continue selling direct to galleries along the coast, where I used to live."

Wow, this woman had moved *after* blindness had set in?

"I'm glad I came back here at my brother's invitation," Trinity went on. "Caleb helped me out a lot. You may have met him? Dale says you were in church Sunday, and my brother leads worship there. Anyway, Caleb helped set up my studio in his garage, which was a huge help, but then I met Dale, and the rest is history."

How could this blind woman look so serene in the sight of... *bad choice of words, Eryn. Even in your own head.* But still, Trinity seemed completely at peace with her lot in life.

She had a beautiful studio and home along the lake that she couldn't see clearly, but she radiated peace.

Where Eryn had second, third, and eighteenth thoughts for everything, always worried about the next thing. Could she find the kind of acceptance and joy Trinity had? Trinity had every reason to be a nervous Nellie, but Eryn was still in first place. Not a race she should aspire to win.

"What does your husband do?"

"Dale and his brother own Communication Location downtown. They sell all kinds of electronic games and gadgets. His brother is a professor over in Butte, so he and his family only live here in the summertime and take over the business for a while so Dale gets a break."

"That sounds nice. Family can be amazing." Not that Eryn would know, though the Sullivans seemed to make it all work.

"They really can." Trinity smiled. "But the family of God is even better. I hope you really connect in with Creekside Fellowship now that you live here. There's nothing like building relationships with fellow believers."

"Thank you for that encouragement." The other woman was right. Eryn should stop massaging that chip on her shoulder — after all, no one here but Maxwell knew Amelia at all — and settle in as though she intended this to be her lifelong home. It might even be true.

CHAPTER SEVENTEEN

I t had been an amazing day, watching Eryn come into her own as she chatted with the artisans she'd selected for the gift shop. She might think there was a chance her proposal to Sweet River's board might be rejected, but Maxwell knew it wouldn't be. Not only because no one else wanted the job, but because she was clearly capable of taking on the challenge.

He pulled into the parking lot at the Chuckwagon Bar & Grill and grinned across the cab at her. "Ready for dinner?"

Eryn bounced a little on her seat. "So ready. It seems a long time since food."

"That's because it was." He laughed and jumped out of the cab. They'd had lunch in Missoula after visiting the candy maker, who was thrilled to be a supplier and even offered to design wrappers specially for the ranch gift shop.

Maxwell opened the passenger door. It had taken most of today's stops to convince Eryn to stay put until he got to her. He held out his hand to help her descend, then kept a firm grip on her fingers as he shut the door and beeped the locks.

Eryn pulled back. "I'm not dressed for a fancy dinner."

"This isn't a fancy place. No worries on that score. They have great ribs and steaks." His stomach rumbled as though on cue. "Just in time."

She laughed and fell in step beside him as they crossed to the front door and then entered. The host ushered them to a table tucked into a bay window with a fireplace nearby. Maxwell seated Eryn.

"I love this!" she murmured. "The trees turning color, the carpet of leaves, the little fountain."

They'd have to request this table for a winter date, when snow would blanket the view and the blazing fireplace would be even more welcome. And again in spring, because weren't those fruit trees? The blossoms would be lovely.

Maxwell wanted to bring her here in every season, over and over again. He couldn't picture his future without her in it. They'd only reconnected a few weeks ago, but he was growing certain that he loved her. Was it too soon to know that?

In his mind's eye, Tate busted a gut laughing.

Okay, maybe not too early, but Eryn wasn't Stephanie. She wasn't chasing him back as determinedly as he was chasing her. Not like Stephanie, who'd seen a good thing in Tate and had been all in from the first minute.

Maxwell hadn't understood his brother's full, deep dive back then. How could a confirmed bachelor like Tate change his mind with the flick of an on-off switch? Of course, there'd been Jamie. Accepting custody of their young nephew had already rocked Tate's world, readying him for love and marriage.

Maxwell hadn't been shaken, not that way. But that didn't mean he wasn't completely enthralled with the woman across the little table from him.

She gazed out the window, looking more relaxed than he'd seen before. Her blond hair hung in loose curls, framing her heart-shaped face, and cascading down her pale green sweater.

He reached over and covered her hand with both of his. "You're beautiful."

"Me?" Her other hand pressed to her chest as her wide eyes met his.

"You." He smiled. "I've never met anyone who affected me the way you do. It's not just your outward beauty — although you have that in spades — but your inner beauty, too. You light up when you're talking about something you're passionate about. I saw that over and over today."

She glanced down at the table before peeking at him again. "I really enjoyed meeting everyone. I was super nervous, because I don't really do people. But they were so nice."

"It helped that you had something to talk about, that you didn't have to chat about the weather or your move from Kansas or whatever." Although those things had come up, of course. The conversations simply had an end game.

"Yes, that helped." She bit her lip. "Thanks for agreeing to come with me today. I know you couldn't really afford to take the day off."

"Nothing came up that Jordan couldn't handle. Yeah, he

phoned a few times, but it was all good." Heather had been with Maxwell long enough that she wouldn't have bothered him for these minor details. She would have made decisions on her own, and it would have been fine, but Jordan didn't have her level of experience. Not yet, anyway.

Time to change the subject. He retrieved his hands to open his menu. "Do you like seafood?"

Eryn looked down and toyed with the linen napkin. "I don't know. I've had popcorn shrimp, and it was okay."

"Right." Maxwell chuckled. "Kansas isn't known for great seafood, not that Montana is coastal, either. Game to try some for an appetizer? They have a sampler platter that looks good."

"Sure."

"And then what's your fancy? They have steak, ribs, and chicken. I've never eaten here—" the Chuckwagon had a reputation as a date place "—but I've heard it's all good."

Eryn opened her menu and scanned the entries. "The smokehouse ribs sound yummy."

Whew, he'd been hoping she wouldn't turn out to be one of those women who pretended they were overweight and dabbled in salads.

"I'll have the Caesar and fries for my sides," she concluded then closed her menu.

"Perfect. I think I'll have the same." He placed their order when the server returned with their drinks then leaned back and studied Eryn. "Are you happy you moved to Montana? I need to ask you before winter, just in case stormy weather makes you change your mind."

Eryn laughed. "Yeah, I think I am glad."

His eyebrows popped upward. "You're not sure? Here I thought you were settling in like this was where you were always meant to be."

"It seems presumptuous to say that when I lived 28 years in the same house a thousand miles away."

Maxwell wanted to know everything about her. "When's your birthday?"

Her gaze flew to meet his. "April fourth. Yours?"

"Uh…" He should have thought that question through. "November 18."

"Just a few weeks away." Eryn eyed him thoughtfully. "Now that you mention it, I do remember you being one of the older kids in our class."

"Yeah." There had been pros and cons to that. Time to cut to the chase. "Eryn? I like you a lot. Would you be willing to go out with me?"

"Isn't that what we're doing right now?"

Wait, was that a tiny smile playing at the edge of her mouth?

He groaned. "Woman, you're killing me. Yes, that's what we're doing right now, but what I'm asking is if you might consider me your boyfriend. This sounds all high school, right? Eryn, would you go steady with me?"

"No one ever asked me that before."

"I haven't asked anyone before."

She peeked up at him. "I find that hard to believe. You seem to have everything together. You're cute, you're confident, you're…"

"Wait, you think I'm cute?"

"Yes?" She peered through her eyelashes.

"Man, I was hoping for an adjective that wouldn't fit

167

Jamie or Simon. Manly. Handsome." He paused, but she didn't fully look at him. He bobbed his eyebrows, hoping she'd catch their motion. "Hot."

Eryn snickered, and her face pinked, but at least she was looking at him now. "Okay, all of those. How did some woman not snap you up already?"

Maxwell sobered. "A few reasons, I guess. I wasn't looking for a relationship before, but also, I… I keep pretty busy, which is a socially acceptable way of saying I'm a workaholic." A long breath whooshed out of him. "My parents — let's just say I take after my father. Every spare minute goes into my work. That's why my parents divorced, because my mother refused to put up with Dad's nonexistent spare time. He had no leftovers for her or for us boys, honestly."

Eryn studied him. "But you moved to Chicago to be with him after high school."

"I did. I couldn't wait to get out of Gilead, to be honest. There was nothing for me there." He chuckled. "I didn't *know* you, even though technically we've known each other since kindergarten."

"No, everyone knew Amelia. Not me."

"I'm sorry." He started to reach for her hands, but the server chose that moment to appear with their seafood platter. Maybe it was time to change the subject, anyway.

"I'M NOT ready for this day to end." Maxwell tangled his fingers with hers as they exited the restaurant.

"Me, either." Dinner had been delicious, even the suspicious-looking mussels. They'd talked about lighter topics over the meal, and for the first time in her entire life, Eryn felt seen for herself. It was a heady feeling.

"Since there isn't a great movie playing, let's go for a walk." He nudged her shoulder toward the park across the street.

Eryn reveled in the heady emotions surging through her. She still couldn't believe that a man like Maxwell had singled her out. She shoved thoughts of her twin's journals out of her mind. Amelia's infatuation had been childish. Just because she'd doodled hearts all around Maxwell's name every time it appeared in her entries didn't mean... Right. Eryn pushed Amelia out of her head.

Lamp posts in the park illuminated the pathways. They strolled beside the pond, and Eryn imagined children feeding ducks there on summer days. Imagined moms sitting on the benches watching their kids on the playground, chatting with each other.

She sighed. Could this ever truly be her life?

"Cold?" Maxwell whipped off his fleece jacket and wrapped it over her shoulders before she'd had a chance to reply.

"Thanks, but now you'll be freezing." Maybe this walk on a late October evening was a bad idea, after all.

"There are other ways to keep warm." Maxwell slipped his arm around her waist and tugged her close to his side.

And... maybe this walk was perfect. She snugged her arm around him and let herself enjoy the closeness as they crossed the lakefront drive and stepped onto the sandy beach. The lake lapped gently at the shore in the moonlight.

"You didn't answer my question before."

Eryn knew she hadn't. "What question was that?"

Maxwell stopped and turned her to face him, both arms looped behind her back. "Will you be my girlfriend? Because I'm falling for you, and I can't get enough time with you."

"What about that whole workaholic thing you mentioned?" She was stalling. She knew it, but she couldn't help drawing out the moment. She wanted to savor this for the rest of her life, even if things ended badly next week.

"I hope I've learned from my father's mistakes." Maxwell's dark eyes were in the shadows, but she could feel the intensity of his gaze even so.

"I'd like to be with you," she whispered, slipping her arms around his neck.

His hands tightened on her back, slowly pulling her closer.

Was he going to kiss her? Was she ready?

"May I?" he whispered.

Forget her inhibitions, her shyness, her inexperience. Eryn rose on her tiptoes and met his lips with her own.

She'd never been kissed. Not even the guy who'd tried to get to Amelia through her had gone this far.

And she was kind of glad that Maxwell was her first, because the feelings for him that had been building up for weeks now were more real than anything she'd ever experienced before.

He deepened the kiss, his hands roving her back then tangling in her hair.

She cupped the back of his head and thrilled at the feel of his curly strands beneath her fingers. As his girlfriend, she had the right to kiss him, to touch him, to enjoy moments such as this.

How could heaven be any better?

No need to consider heaven right now, either. Just Maxwell and the thought that he cared about her. Not just a thought. He was proving that this wasn't a figment of her imagination, that someone could care about her, because she, Eryn Ann Ralston, was worthy.

Heady knowledge.

CHAPTER EIGHTEEN

W hat's with the boss man?" Tory stage-whispered to Janessa. "He hasn't stopped smiling all morning."

Maxwell turned and gave his worker a mock glare. "I've smiled before."

"Once a day, whether he needs to or not," quipped Janessa. "Just kidding, boss."

"Hey, I'm not that bad." Was he? He didn't think so.

"Nah, just focused. It's all good."

Janessa had been with the team since their move to Montana, and Heather had trained her in her current capacities. Had Heather thought he was too focused? Was that why she'd turned in her notice back in spring? She'd said it was because she'd met someone back home. She'd introduced her fiancé to Maxwell at Graham and Cadence's wedding in September and told him she hoped he'd attend their spring wedding.

He'd wondered for a while after she left if he'd missed a cue because work consumed all his mental energy. Might he have captured Heather's attention and love if he'd been more available, more watchful? The question paralleled that of his parents'. Dad had let their marriage slip from inattention. Work had been his mistress. Still was.

Maxwell shook his head. Meeting Eryn had made him thankful Heather had left on amicable terms. He'd never felt for Heather a fraction of how he felt for Eryn, but the worry still niggled that he had too much of his father's nature in him. How did a guy keep his life in balance?

"...lost in his own little world," Janessa continued.

Maxwell snapped to attention. "Okay, does anyone have questions about your tasks for today, or is this just pick-on-Maxwell hour? We've got deadlines on this project, so hop to it."

"I've added paint to the next pick-up at the hardware store," Janessa said. "We'll be running out of Foggy Forest by the end of the day, and I'll need more for Cottage Four."

"I saw that." Jordan nodded. "I need more drywall screws and another #2 bit, along with drywall for Cottage Six. If anyone has anything to add, I'll get a delivery up here for tomorrow morning."

"I'll double-check the other paint supplies." Janessa dusted her hands together.

"Steve?"

The tiler frowned at Janessa. "I think I'm good on tiles and grout for the next two bathrooms, but I'll check."

See? This crew all but ran itself. They didn't even really need Maxwell.

As the group dispersed from their informal meeting, Janessa stopped beside him, her eyes twinkling. "Have a good date yesterday, boss?"

"Sure did. And I don't feel the slightest bit of guilt for ditching you all to keep working while I took a day off."

"And why should you?"

"Why should I feel guilty?" Maxwell stared at her. "Because I pride myself on working harder than the rest of you put together."

She smirked. "You do that, anyway. How many hours have you put in on the treehouse designs, and we won't even start building for six months?"

"Uh… lots." Innumerable, in fact. "But that doesn't count, because it's not today's boots-on-the-ground project."

"The treehouses will *never* be boots on the ground, boss."

Maxwell reared back. "You don't think they're viable? I assure you, they totally are. There's this place in Oregon—"

Janessa smacked his arm. "It'll be boots in the sky. Treehouses aren't on the ground. Sheesh, I can't believe I had to explain that to you."

"There's a jokester in every crowd." Maxwell rolled his eyes. "Didn't you say you had a ton of painting to do today?"

"Sure do, but I can't pass up the chance to check in with you."

He stared at her. Was she insinuating—?

"Not like that, Maxwell the Great. Good grief. One woman bats her eyelashes at you, and you think the entire female race wants to elbow her out of the way and have their chance with you." She walked away.

"Janessa?"

She turned back, eyebrows lifted. "Did I go too far?"

"Kind of." Dad certainly would have fired her on the spot for impertinence and lack of respect for authority, but Maxwell hadn't run his business that way. He'd focused on running a tight ship but with camaraderie. Didn't a little razzing count for that? "Do you really think I'm full of myself?"

Janessa eyed him. "Not in a bad way," she said at last.

"Is there any other way?"

"Sorry, boss. I shouldn't have pushed your buttons. The paintbrush is calling me."

Maxwell let her go but couldn't get her words out of his head. He was confident, at least in his business decisions. Less so with women, but then they'd never factored into his life until recently, so he had less experience there. He'd felt like he was finding his footing with Eryn as of last night — that kiss! — but had he seemed too cocky to her, too? Did she feel, like Janessa seemed to, that she needed to fall in line because Maxwell the Great expected it, and it was easier not to resist?

Eryn *had* resisted, though, unless she'd previously been oblivious to his hints of interest over the past few weeks. Okay, they hadn't been hints. He'd been fairly straightforward with her from the beginning, as direct as he dared to be before fearing she'd bolt the opposite direction.

Maxwell was accustomed to getting what he wanted. Outbidding his opponents by a dollar? Check. Subcontractors working overtime to meet his deadlines? Check. Designing treehouses for a resort in Montana? Check. Getting the woman of his dreams to look at him with stars in her eyes? Check.

He stared out the window of Cottage Four toward the small lake, where a light drizzle pebbled the gray surface.

Could he *keep* Eryn's attention? Not by manipulation or by force. She had to want him — want them as a couple — as much as he did. And she wouldn't if she saw him like Janessa did, as a conceited but hopefully benevolent dictator.

He couldn't boss Eryn around. She wasn't his employee. But he didn't know any other way to get results. It worked in every other area of life, more or less. And if he'd lost a few times because he'd overstepped, it was no big problem. There was always some other solution.

But not with Eryn. If he lost with her, he'd lost his future. That wasn't a gamble he was willing to take.

Lord, help him, he had to do this right the first time.

DAD WAS PROBABLY WORKING out at the farm, and Maxwell was in one of the houses on Ladybug Lane. Eryn hadn't explored out that direction yet, but she didn't want to disturb him at work. Didn't want his crew to snicker that she was chasing him if she showed up there for a tour as though it were her right.

She'd written up her notes on all the artisans they'd met yesterday and doodled a layout for the gift shop based on those considerations. But she was restless, tired of thinking about all that.

Work on her quilt design for the ranch? No. Her sketch was too simplistic, too amateur compared to what real artists brought to the table. Did she have enough scraps for a prototype? She'd need to get her sewing machines and notions out of their storage boxes stacked in the loft. It would be better to do that after she and Dad had moved into the farmhouse. Only a couple of weeks to go, if she could wait that long.

Maxwell had divulged his birthday, and it was coming up soon. What was a proper gift for someone in a new relationship? She was probably going to mess this up. Was there anyone she could ask for advice?

In her mind's eye, her twin mocked her.

But Amelia wasn't here. If she'd still been alive, Eryn and Dad wouldn't have moved to Montana. Amelia would have gone to the reunion and caught Maxwell's eye. After all, he'd been looking for her. He probably remembered their childhood dalliance, too.

Paisley? But Paisley was as outgoing as Eryn was shy. Would any good advice she might offer be worth Eryn putting herself out there?

There was no other way to make friends. Eryn'd had so few of those all her life. Most had been appropriated by Amelia, and Eryn hadn't fought back. How had she been such a doormat?

Eryn opened her phone. Paisley had put her number in it back that first day and had texted a few times, but Eryn had never initiated a conversation. She was such a loser.

Now, though…

Eryn: *Hi! What are you up to this afternoon?*

Paisley: *I'm in the office down at the lodge, but I could sure use a break. Want to come down?*

It was gray and rainy outside, so indoors was preferred, and someone had started a fire in the lodge's great room fireplace this morning while Eryn was kneading bread. It had looked inviting but, on the other hand, they could be overheard by anyone passing through the lodge.

And she was being a coward. Again.

Eryn: *Sure. When's good?*

Paisley: *Anytime. Just come to my office when you get here.*

Eryn: *Okay.*

She looked around the little duplex, which was tidy and impersonal with few of their own belongings in view. Then she slipped on her boots and rain jacket and grabbed her umbrella. She tucked her phone and knit slippers in her pockets and headed out the door.

This cluster of staff duplexes must feel like a real community in the heat of summer when every unit was stuffed with workers. Now, many sat vacant or had only one occupant, like Paisley's.

Even in the late October drizzle, the ranch was pretty. The leaves had fallen and been raked away or been pummeled into nearly colorless, sodden blobs along the roadway. The lake lay gray today with wisps of fog hovering overtop, the mountains around them obscured by low clouds.

The vibe was still completely different than Kansas. The rain fell downward instead of sideways, to start with. The lack of blasting wind was a pleasure.

Eryn passed the corner to Pegasus Lane and walked the rest of the way down the hill to the lodge with its wisps of wood smoke rising from the stone chimney. The huge log building with its wide covered decks and impressive views never failed to amaze her. How was this her life?

She was so lucky — no, blessed — to live here now. To be dating Maxwell Sullivan.

Yeah, she needed Paisley's advice on that score. She shook out her umbrella and closed it before heading in the door to the office wing. She hung it on a hook and removed her wet boots, pulling her slippers out of her pockets then putting them on. She rapped lightly on Paisley's door.

"Come on in!"

Eryn poked her head inside and blinked at the plethora of stuff smothering every surface. The walls were lined with whiteboards and bulletin boards covered with doodles and charts and business cards and brochures. A bouquet of balloons trailing ribbons was tacked to the corner of a half-empty shelving unit, the contents of which appeared to have erupted across a folding table in the middle.

This was a scary place, but it seemed to work for Paisley. It would never work for Eryn.

"Let me just wrap this up." Paisley's fingers danced over her keyboard.

"Want a hot chocolate? I can make a couple and meet you by the fireplace." There certainly wasn't any place to sit in here.

"Oh, perfect! I'd love that. I just need two minutes."

Which would probably be five or ten, but that was okay. Eryn had nowhere else to be. She backed out and headed into the dining area.

Nadine glanced up from deep in the kitchen. "Hey there!"

"Hi. I just want to get a couple of hot chocolates if that's okay." She indicated the machine next to the coffee carafes.

"Sure. Are you meeting Maxwell?"

"No, Paisley."

"Oh." Nadine seemed disappointed. "There are cookies out for snack time, so help yourself. Thanks for making them."

Eryn smiled. "Part of my job."

"And everyone is thankful." Nadine chuckled. "Having your help is making things easier. I hadn't realized how barebones things got around here over the winter."

"Oh. You're welcome." It was nice to be seen as more than a pity project. Eryn fixed two mugs of hot chocolate and set them on a tray along with four chocolate chip cookies. She carried the tray into the great room and rested it on a live-edge end table.

"Hey, thanks. You shouldn't have." Bryce dropped into the chair on the other side and reached for a mug.

"I... uh..."

"Oh, no. Are you expecting my brother?" Bryce's hand hovered above the tray as he looked at her with eyebrows raised.

"No. Paisley."

"Oh, in *that* case..." He rolled his eyes and rose to his feet. "I never hang around where I'm not wanted. But, you know, when you get tired of stick-in-the-mud Maxie, you know where to find me. I'm the fun one."

If Bryce awaited a reply, he wasn't going to get one. Eryn remained standing beside the end table and stared at him, keeping her expression as impassive as humanly possible.

"Fine. I get it." He backed away, both palms toward her. "You think that won't happen, but it would take a miracle, you know. All he knows how to do is snap his fingers and make things happen. It gets old." Bryce pivoted and strolled away, whistling.

Paisley jogged around the corner and dodged around Bryce before dropping into the seat he'd vacated. "What was that all about? Mmm, chocolate chip cookies. My favorite."

"Bryce?" Eryn was trembling as she lowered herself into the other chair. "He was… flirting?" Guys didn't flirt with her. And if this was what it was like, she hoped one never did again.

"The jerk can't help it." Paisley shook her head. "I'm glad you texted me. I needed a break in the worst way. What's up?"

Eryn, you need a girlfriend. Just spit it out.

"It's Maxwell's birthday in a couple of weeks, and I don't know what to do."

Paisley's face brightened. "Oh, girl, you have come to the right place."

CHAPTER NINETEEN

M axwell arrived in the dining hall minutes
before the line closed. He'd meant to arrive
sooner. Of course, he had. He had a girlfriend
to eat meals with now, but Jordan had pulled him aside at
the end of the workday to point out that the tiles for
Cottage Three had come from two different dye lots and
didn't exactly match. By the time Maxwell had phoned the
supplier and made arrangements for half a dozen boxes to
be replaced, it was 5:55 instead of 5:15.

He scanned the dining hall as he stood behind Jordan,
who was divvying the last of the baked beans onto two
plates. His heart leaped when he saw Eryn and her dad
sitting with Paisley and Weston. Oh, and Bryce. What was
Bryce doing there? Up to no good, for sure.

After loading up his tray, Maxwell headed toward their
table. There was no vacant spot beside Eryn, so he took the
seat between Bryce and Weston. "Hey, sorry I'm late."

"You'll be late for your own funeral," Bryce quipped.
"Too busy *working*." He finger-quoted that.

Slugging his brother would be super satisfying. Maxwell did his best to even his tone. "Hey, someone around here has to do their job."

Bryce leaned back in his chair. "We all do our job. Even me, believe it or not."

"Congratulations." Maxwell ducked his head for a silent grace. Was it okay to ask God to shut his brother up along with being thankful for food? He'd take a chance on protocol.

"So, how was your day?" Maxwell glanced around the table before resting his gaze on Eryn.

"Not bad," Bryce put in. "I planted ten pounds of crocus bulbs in that bed in the campground. Should be a nice pop of color come spring."

"Good for you." Maxwell shot an irritated look at his brother. "Eryn?"

She glanced between them, a slight frown marring her features. "Nadine is teaching me the ways of sourdough bread. I also baked cookies this morning."

"Best chocolate chip cookies I've ever tasted," Bryce said. "Did you get any, Maxie? Oh, wait. I bet you were too busy to come down for afternoon coffee."

"It's Nadine's recipe," Eryn said.

"She doesn't have your touch." Bryce smirked. "Truly amazing. Didn't you think so, Paisley?"

"What I think is that you should shut your face." Paisley glowered at him.

"Hear, hear," Maxwell said under his breath.

"Stop mumbling, little brother. Didn't Mom teach you to speak up? Wait, no. That was Dad. Take charge of your words, Maxie."

Maxie? Seriously? Was Bryce ready for his head to roll? Also, how had this become Maxwell's life? He was late, sure, but that didn't usually put him off his game. But then Bryce didn't usually pick on him so blatantly.

Was Bryce seriously hitting on Eryn? She wasn't his type. If she were, she wouldn't be attractive to Maxwell. Plain and simple. Therefore, he must be doing it merely to annoy Maxwell. And it was working.

Maxwell studied his brother.

Bryce met his gaze with an eyebrow lifted in challenge.

"These baked beans smell great." Maxwell shoveled in a bite and tossed a prayer heavenward that he wouldn't lose his cool and deck his big brother right there in the dining hall. He could totally take him, though. Right? Although Bryce had been digging and raking and edging and whatever landscapers did for a couple of summers. He might have grown a muscle or two.

Doubtful, but possible. Either way, this wasn't the time to find out.

"Hey, Maxwell." Paisley pushed her plate aside as she leaned on the table. "A few of us are talking about heading out on a trail ride slash camping trip the weekend before Thanksgiving up to that mountain lake. Interested?"

Maxwell's fork stopped halfway to his mouth. "Sounds cold." Still, would Eryn be going? He glanced toward her, but she was looking down.

"Yeah, I agree." Bryce punched Maxwell's shoulder a little harder than required. "We Sullivans are used to the lap of luxury, and camping in the mountains in November is not remotely luxurious."

"No one invited you." Paisley skewered him with a look. "I was talking to Maxwell."

Whoa, Maxwell hadn't realized how deeply Paisley's animosity toward his brother ran. Had Bryce tried to lure Paisley into his web before she'd caught up with Weston? Probably. She was female, under 50, and lived in Montana.

And now he was hitting on Eryn. Not because he wanted her — probably — so it must be to mess with Maxwell. What had Max ever done to him to deserve this treatment? Nothing.

Being born last in a family of four boys meant that Maxwell had scrambled for every bit of favor from his father. As eldest and heir to the Sullivan throne, Wally'd had the lion's share of approval. Easygoing but hardworking, Tate had been Mama's boy while holding his own with Dad.

Bryce had been an underachiever his entire life. It hadn't taken Maxwell long to realize he might never be either parent's favorite, but he could beat out Bryce with one hand tied behind his back.

Had Bryce resented that? No one had made him step aside.

And now it seemed he wasn't taking it anymore, but petty digs and jealousy games were juvenile maneuvers unsuiting to a Sullivan.

Maxwell nearly choked on his mouthful of ham. Oh, boy. When had he gotten as conceited as Janessa's earlier accusation? Because he seemed to think that Sullivans were above mere mortals.

Except for Bryce.

Whoa, he had some thinking and praying to do.

DINNER HAD BEEN AGONIZING. Maxwell had been late, and his brother rude and condescending. If that was flirting, Eryn wanted none of it. Paisley's invitation to the trail ride had fizzled. Weston, as usual, was lost in his own quiet world, and Dad had yawned repeatedly throughout the meal and excused himself before everyone else was finished.

That would leave Eryn to walk back to staff housing with Maxwell. She should be glad of that, right? They'd been together for only a couple of days, but other than that one perfect kiss, nothing had changed.

Seriously, Eryn? You expected him to ditch his job for you every day like he did Monday? He has work to do. Work he hasn't invited you to see. Work with several female crew members. Also, Janessa is pretty.

Eryn shook her head, trying to dislodge the insidious thoughts. Would she ever feel worthy of anything, let alone Maxwell's attention?

The attention he hadn't given her today.

Because he was working, as he should.

"Deep in thought?" Maxwell smiled at her across the table.

Bryce elbowed his brother. "Not sure how you'd even know about that. Your brainwaves are so shallow they barely exist."

And Eryn was so, so tired of listening to Bryce cut Maxwell down.

Paisley pulled Weston to his feet and turned to Eryn. "See you tomorrow!"

"Sure!" Eryn infused brightness into her tone. Could she walk back with Paisley and Weston instead? No, not with the way Weston pecked a kiss to Paisley's cheek then tugged her toward the doors.

Maybe she could go in the kitchen and help Nadine wind down the day, but the lights were already low beyond the counters.

What kind of woman wanted to get away from her boyfriend? But it wasn't Maxwell she wanted to avoid, it was Bryce, who seemed to enjoy nothing more than jabbing a stick in the spokes of their fledgling relationship.

Carrying his half-finished plate, Maxwell rounded the table and slid into Paisley's deserted seat. "I missed you today," he said quietly.

Eryn caught Bryce's eyeroll from the corner of her eye, but she'd do her best to ignore him if Maxwell did. "I missed you, too."

"Get any more done on the proposal?"

"A bit. I could show you a sketch later."

He grinned at her. "I'd like that."

"I'd like that," Bryce echoed in a mocking tone.

Maxwell turned to his brother. "Don't you have a life of your own? Because you've overstayed your welcome around here."

"The dining hall is a public space."

Maxwell shook his head and ate several more bites before rising. "I think I've had enough. Are you ready to go?"

Eryn eyed his plate. "You don't want your dinner?"

"Seems my appetite has fled." He glanced toward his brother.

Bryce smirked.

"I'm good sitting here until you're done. You've worked hard today and need your calories."

Maxwell stood beside his chair, clearly undecided.

"You two are just too cute," Bryce mocked as he stood up. "I know when I'm not wanted."

"Do you?" Maxwell stared him down across the table.

"Definitely, but you make it entirely too amusing to take you seriously. I'll be going now. Don't worry. I'll see you around." Bryce sauntered off.

Maxwell released a long breath but didn't reseat himself until the lodge doors closed. "Sorry."

"He's your brother. He's not you." Words Eryn should take to heart in her own life.

"I know, but still. He's mostly ignored me forever, and I'm not sure how I got a target plastered on my back now."

Had Eryn underestimated Bryce? Was he actually jealous of Maxwell because of her? No. Couldn't be. She wasn't that special.

Maxwell pushed the remaining food around his plate and shook his head. "I wasn't completely kidding about my appetite having disappeared."

"I'm sorry."

"It's not your fault. I can only blame Bryce for that. He makes everything seem so unpalatable."

Bryce being at their table and mocking Maxwell *was* Eryn's fault, though, but there wasn't any point in arguing about it. "I don't want to talk about your brother."

Maxwell grimaced. "Me, either. I finally have my sweet girl to myself, and all I can talk about is my petty sibling?

Smooth move, Sullivan." He caught Eryn's eye and offered a self-deprecating smile.

"What did you think of Paisley's idea for a trail ride up to the lake? She showed me some photos from their camping trip there last summer."

"It's November. We'd be lucky if the trail wasn't covered in snow."

"It's in ten days, and the forecast says it will stay unseasonably warm at least that long."

He eyed her. "You really want to go?"

This had been Paisley's big idea for a surprise party for Maxwell. Eryn might have misgivings, but the outcome would be worth it, right? She still didn't know what she'd give him for a gift — what did you get a man who had enough money to buy whatever he wanted? No clue. "It sounds fun?"

Maxwell shook his head and laughed. "I never thought you'd be a diehard outdoorswoman, but if you want to go and it's not snowing up there, sure, I'm game."

"Paisley says it's a really nice spot and there are two pit toilets and a campfire ring and everything."

"A really nice spot in July." Maxwell chuckled and raised both hands in surrender. "No, I said I'm game, and I am. Did she say if there are any hot springs in that area?"

"Hot springs?"

"Montana has loads of them, but I'm sure she'd have mentioned if there was one. I was teasing." He scraped the remaining food to one edge of his plate. "I hate to dump this, but I will, anyway. Ready to go?"

"I'll clean our table so it's ready for morning."

"Okay." He carried their plates and cutlery into the

kitchen and added them to the small stack awaiting morning while she snagged a spray bottle and a cloth to wipe the last couple of tables.

She put the supplies away to find him waiting for her. "Ready?"

"Sure."

Maxwell ushered her out of the lodge and paused on the wide front steps. "Listen."

"What am I listening for?"

He tugged her to his side. "What do you hear?"

Not much. "An owl."

"The wind in the treetops. Anything else?"

Distant laughter from up on Hummingbird Lane. A door shutting. "It's so quiet."

"I love it. I hadn't realized how desensitized I'd been to the sounds of nature living in Chicago so many years."

Memories of the Kansas farm flooded Eryn. The horses Dad sold along with the sleigh after Mom died. The smell of prairie grasses in spring and of the wheat harvest in late summer. The blue, blue skies and puffy clouds and the shelter belt of trees around the farmhouse, alive with songbirds and small mammals. The breeze — occasionally hurricane-force — that swirled her hair away from her face and cleared the cobwebs from her brain.

She leaned against Maxwell. "Kansas wasn't noisy."

"You're right. Not like Chicago, but we lived in town limits and not really in tune with nature. This—" he waved his free arm "—this all is something I never knew I needed in my life. I didn't want to need it."

"Too busy to need it?"

He scoffed lightly. "You've been listening to Bryce too

much. Sure, I kept busy, but not too busy to be aware of my surroundings. It's the entire pace of life here that's different. The sounds around us are only an indication. No traffic and sirens and gunshots, just stillness."

The owl hooted again and was answered by another across the lake.

"And owls." Maxwell laughed. "Let's walk. It's freezing."

Eryn tucked her arm around his waist and reveled in the embrace of his arm around her. Yes, he was busy and often late to meals. Yes, he had a rude brother. But moments like this made it worthwhile.

They hiked up the hill to where several lanes diverged then Maxwell stopped and turned her to look back down the way they'd come. The rising moon shone a path across the small lake and illuminated the dimly lit lodge.

He took her face between his hands and planted a gentle kiss on her lips.

Oh, yes. Moments like this made it *all* worthwhile.

CHAPTER TWENTY

H
ey, kids. Want a cup of tea?" Eryn's dad stood by the counter, kettle in hand, as Maxwell ushered Eryn into the duplex the Ralstons shared.

"Good evening, Keith." Maxwell toed off his damp shoes. "Sure, sounds good. Eryn?"

She unzipped her jacket, and Maxwell slid it off her shoulders and hung it before removing his own.

"Sure." She smiled at her father. "Thanks, Dad."

Keith reached into the cupboard for two more mismatched mugs.

"How are things going up at the farm?"

Yeah, Maxwell knew the farming operations were part of the ranch and not their own thing, but they were more behind the scenes. Some dude ranches brought roping and roundups to the forefront and let tourists experience the whole range of ranching life, but Sweet River Ranch had been more of a resort when Grandfather bought it.

Weston hadn't pushed for inclusion. They'd been too

short-staffed, at least with the kind of seasoned cowboys that could handle the confluence of cattle and tourists.

Meanwhile, they'd kept the cows, since Joseph had been instated for over a decade and knew what he was doing. Plus, there was all the rangeland, and it seemed wasteful not to put it to good use. The cow-calf operation paid for itself and brought in some extra.

"The farm is going well. We shipped a couple of truck-loads of calves a few days ago, so the workload is down. But it will increase when the snow flies and Joseph is gone." Keith shook his head. "My dad made the shift from a mixed farm to wheat when I was a young'un, so I don't know cows real well. I hope your family hasn't put your trust in the wrong farmer."

Maxwell hoped the same, since hiring Keith had been his suggestion. "There are ranchers nearby who can give advice or a hand if you need it. Declan Cavanagh just up the road at Rockstead has a solid reputation. He or one of his boys would likely be happy to answer questions."

"Good to know. Joseph said the same. He'll be down in Jewel Lake, so not too far if I'm in over my head."

The kettle boiled, and Keith poured hot water into the three mugs.

Maxwell touched the small of Eryn's back and guided her to the table. It wasn't like he'd stopped by to chat with her father, but being on the man's good side was preferable.

"One thing I find interesting around here is how much is secured with just a handshake." Keith set the honey bear and a jar of dry creamer on the table along with three spoons.

Maxwell eyed the creamer. Not a chance was he dumping those chemicals in his tea. "Sullivan Enterprises runs on signed legal contracts." As did his construction company.

"Oh, I didn't mean it in a haphazard way. Just if someone says he'll do something and shakes on it, everyone considers it done."

"Well, yes." Maxwell chuckled. "If that's a new concept, you've been hanging out with the wrong crowd."

"I guess I got took a few times and got wary." Keith nudged the honey bear across the table. "Here you go, Rynie."

She eyed her dad. "By whom? Larry Groening?"

That was the man who'd bought their farm to save them from bankruptcy, right? The market farmer next door?

"Oh, I didn't mean Larry. He's definitely one of the good ones. In a town built around a Bible college, you'd think there would be more like him."

"My grandfather and my father always taught me that a man's word is his bond. If you promise something, you deliver it faster and better than your word. You can't run a hotel empire like Sullivan on handshakes alone, but the addition of a notarized signature only seals what we've already said." Maxwell shrugged and squeezed a little honey into his tea. "We strive to make the written agreement match the verbal one... and then outdo them both."

"Commendable." Keith heaped creamer into his cup and stirred.

Maxwell tried not to wince.

"So, your aunt..."

"Beatrice is the company lawyer. She—" Duh. That wasn't the aunt Keith was talking about. Graham's parents, Theodore and Beatrice, hadn't been to the ranch since the wedding, just before the Ralstons had arrived.

Keith frowned. "Beatrice?"

"I'm sorry. I'm not used to Nadine being my aunt yet, but that's whom you meant."

"Right. Sorry." Keith chuckled. "She seems really nice."

Maxwell managed not to grin. "I've found the same thing." He was going to make Eryn's dad strive for every word, though. "What do you think of her, Eryn? You've been working with her for over a week."

"She's teaching me to make sourdough bread!"

"There you have it." Maxwell chuckled. "The highest praise possible. Her bread is amazing... another reason I'm not moving back to Chicago any time soon. She's spoiled me."

"Oh?" Keith's eyebrows rose as he glanced between Maxwell and Eryn. "I didn't realize you still thought of Chicago as home."

"I don't know that I do, but it was home for the better part of a decade, and I've kept my condo there. I've had to rely on some of my suppliers even now, since all the options I'm accustomed to aren't at my fingertips here. Other than that, Montana is growing on me."

"I was hoping you weren't pulling a bait-and-switch on my daughter. She's been through enough."

"Dad!"

Maxwell reached for Eryn's hand under the table and gave it a squeeze. "No, sir. I'm quite attached to both Montana and to your daughter."

A flush shot up Eryn's cheeks, and she looked down.

"But you've kept your condo?" Keith looked between them. "I feel it's my duty as her father to make sure you're not toying with her."

"I would never."

"Dad, I'm right here. Don't talk about me as though I'm not."

"Rynie, I know you're taken by this guy, but you don't have a lot of experience to judge him by. Dave was—"

"Dad!" Eryn shot to her feet, dropping Maxwell's hand. "Just because I'm not Amelia doesn't mean I'm gullible."

Just who was Dave?

"Amelia?" Keith's brows pulled together as he frowned. "What does she have to do with this? She's not part of this."

"She had a crush on Maxwell when we were all kids."

"I didn't know you two confided in each other."

Wait, what? Maxwell had figured that the twins hadn't been all that close, but if her father assumed they wouldn't have talked about boys they liked, it had to be worse than he'd thought. But maybe it had been obvious. Amelia's fixation on Maxwell had lasted well into high school before she figured out she might as well date other guys, since he wasn't asking. He'd even turned her down for the Sadie Hawkins dance their sophomore year.

Keith shook his head, looking confused. "That's not what I meant."

"It doesn't matter what you meant. You don't need to announce to anyone, let alone Maxwell, how little I've dated."

"I'm sorry, Rynie. I didn't mean it that way." He grimaced into his teacup. "You know, I think I'll just go to bed. I don't know if it's the altitude or the early mornings around here, but I'm about done for."

"I should head out, too." Maxwell rose as Keith did and reclaimed Eryn's hand. Whatever mood they'd built during the stroll from the lodge was well and truly gone. Bryce had ruined dinner... okay, maybe Maxwell had done that himself by being late. And now Keith's seemingly well-intentioned comment soured this moment.

Keith's gaze lingered on his daughter for a moment, solidifying Maxwell's realization he was the third wheel and needed to give them time to clear the air without him overhearing any more. Then Keith disappeared into the bathroom and shut the door.

"Hey." Maxwell turned to Eryn and slid his hands around her waist. "Don't worry about your dad. I think a father's job to take care of his kids never ends." Not that James Sullivan was that sort, but Maxwell could see the tendency in most of the men he knew. He dropped a gentle kiss on Eryn's lips. "I'll see you tomorrow, okay?"

"Okay." Her gaze ricocheted off his as she bit off a sigh.

Man, he hated to leave her like this, but what could he do? She needed to convince her dad she was an adult capable of making her own choices. Given their family history, that would likely take more than one conversation, and Maxwell couldn't do anything to help.

He hated having his hands tied. He was a guy who made things happen.

COULD this evening have been more of a disaster?

Eryn lowered herself back into the chair after Maxwell left and cradled her inflamed face in her hands. Oh, the mortification.

The bathroom door opened, and footsteps approached. "Eryn?"

"How could you, Dad? I feel like I'm 13 again."

"I'm sorry."

"Why? That's all I want to know. Why did you feel the need to humiliate me like that?"

"I didn't realize." Dad sighed. "It's just… I didn't realize back in Kansas just how powerful this family is. Maxwell getting me this job seemed like a nice gesture. Sure, I knew they were rich. I mean, there have been Sullivans in Gilead for decades, but men raised in so much luxury have certain expectations of young women—"

"You're mixing Maxwell up with Bryce."

"Maybe." Dad gripped Eryn's shoulder. "I wanted to send him a message that he can't get away with hurting my little girl. You're all I have left."

"So, you decided to hurt me to prevent *him* from hurting me?" She jerked away from his grasp and stood facing him. "That's all kinds of messed up."

"He needs to think twice," Dad retorted obstinately. "You heard what he said about keeping his home in Chicago."

Eryn shoved the thought aside, though it had jolted her, too. "I'm going to bed, unless you want me to tell you all the reasons not to look at Nadine the way you do. She's part of that family, too, you know."

"She didn't grow up spoiled by all their money."

"It doesn't stop her from having access to it now. And

Maxwell isn't spoiled. He could have had everything fed to him on a silver spoon like Bryce, but he started his own business and worked for it."

"He does seem to be a more upright man than his brother."

"Exactly." Eryn marched into the bathroom and, when she came out a few minutes later, Dad had gone into his bedroom. She mounted the ladder to the loft, still fuming.

Read the Bible or more of Amelia's journals? She didn't want to be comforted or challenged, so why not poke at her childhood to see if it still hurt?

Okay, that thinking was just as mixed up as the whole evening had been. Still, Eryn changed into her pajamas and pulled the top journal out of her drawer. Where was she? She'd read Amelia's thoughts on their mother's death a couple of nights ago, and for the first time in forever, she'd felt a kinship with her twin.

Amelia had grieved, as Eryn had. They'd both lost their mom at a vulnerable age.

November 18, 2008

It's Max's birthday today, and he's 14 now. Practically an adult! [three heart emojis]

Eryn stilled. Amelia had known Maxwell's birthday? Not that it would have been a huge secret, most likely, but Eryn hadn't remembered it. She turned back to the text.

I told him how sad I was about Mom's death. I even cried a little, and he did what I wanted him to do! He gave me a hug and said he was sorry.

Eryn glowered at the page. She really should have burned the journals before they moved. She might have blasted Dad for bringing Amelia into the conversation, but she was just as guilty, since she kept inviting her twin's juvenile thoughts into her current life.

I said I was worried about being alone someday (Eryn doesn't count) and asked if he'd marry me if we got old, like 30, and no one else had. I knew it was a silly thing to ask, but he said, sure, why not?

Does that make me engaged to Maxwell Sullivan at age 13? [three heart emojis] Am I supposed to try to find some other guy to marry later or hold out for him? I should have said 25! Or maybe 21, because I doubt I'll ever meet anyone as dreamy as Max. [heart eye emoji]

Eryn slapped the cover shut and surged to her feet. The loft wasn't very big. It took only 11 steps to get to the other end. And back. And forth. She couldn't believe the gall of her sister, playing off Maxwell's sympathy after Mom's death. Then there was that whole bit about Eryn not counting. What did that even mean? Yeah, they hadn't been close, but had Amelia said those words to Maxwell? Had she actually verbalized, "I feel so alone, and Eryn doesn't count."? Or was it merely an aside in her journal?

Oh, the humiliation. The pain of being the annoying sister. All Eryn had ever wanted was to be friends with her twin. She'd been rebuffed at every turn, from her earliest memories on, until she'd mostly stopped trying.

She remembered reaching for Amelia at Mom's funeral, but her sister had sidestepped her and turned away, doubling Eryn's pain that horrible day.

And tonight, the stab of Amelia's knife twisted again.

What did Maxwell say repeatedly? How his word was his bond. That if he said he'd do something, consider it done.

Did he remember the promise he'd made to Amelia 15 years ago? Sure, it was no longer valid, since Amelia was dead, but would she have beckoned him with her pinky and reminded him of their marriage pact? Would Mr. Keeps-His-Promises have made good on it? Could Maxwell Sullivan have become Amelia's husband? Eryn's brother-in-law?

Eryn couldn't have this sort of attachment, these feelings, for her brother-in-law. Not that he'd married Amelia or even been in contact most of those years, but the fact that he'd made this sort of promise even as a kid made Eryn's stomach turn.

What now?

She'd never sleep. There was no point in even trying.

She was 28 years old, still lingering in her dead sister's shadow. How could she kiss the man who'd made promises to her twin?

CHAPTER TWENTY-ONE

Eryn was focused on flipping pancakes the next morning when Maxwell entered the dining hall. She was still busy at the back of the kitchen when he realized he was late to the worksites on Ladybug Lane.

It wasn't the first time they hadn't connected at breakfast, though hadn't she always sent him a shy smile before? Today, of all days, he needed some reassurance that she was okay. That she and her dad had talked, and Keith had realized Maxwell was a good guy who wouldn't hurt his daughter.

Not on purpose, anyway.

A guy could make all the promises he wanted, but not everything was within his control. In the construction business, Maxwell was accustomed to switching gears on the fly. A truckload of damaged flooring? Find something else. Something better. A window factory burning to the ground? Shift to the other connections he'd made. He was used to making things happen.

Making things happen should be Maxwell's tagline. He might look into adding it to his business cards.

Eryn stood with her back to the dining hall, talking with Nadine, when Maxwell headed out. He didn't want to interrupt her at work, so he didn't call a goodbye.

They'd talk later. Everything would work out, right? Right.

He was smart enough to know that life was full of twists and turns and that, sooner or later, he and Eryn would need to figure out how to navigate those. He hadn't expected it quite this soon, and he hadn't thought it would be Keith pushing back the way he had.

What was going on there?

Maxwell scratched his head as he drove up to Ladybug Lane and stopped in front of Cottage Four.

Janessa and Steve stood toe to toe and nose to nose as they yelled at each other.

He didn't even need to be able to hear to know their personalities were clashing yet again. In a perverse way, he was glad to be greeted by a situation he could take his frustrations out on.

Careful, Sullivan. You need them both. You need them happy.

Did he, though?

He leaped out of his truck and slammed the door. "What's going on here?" he barked as he strode nearer.

"Boss man, he—"

"Thank God you're here, Maxwell. She's completely whacko."

Perfect. Maxwell was itching for a fight.

He pointed at Janessa. "You. Come with me and tell me what's going on. You—" he pointed at Steve "—find something useful to do. I'll be with you in a few minutes. Got it?"

Janessa's chin came up as she sent one more dagger glare at Steve. "Yes, sir."

"Whatever." Steve's glower at Janessa remained unabated.

Maxwell stepped in front of Steve. "Excuse me?"

"Yes, sir." But the guy didn't look happy about it.

That made three of them. Maxwell gestured toward his truck. It offered privacy in clear view of anyone who cared, including Steve. "Janessa?" He held the passenger door.

She climbed in with a huff and crossed her arms over her chest. "That is a moron who cannot read directions."

Maxwell settled in the driver's seat and closed his eyes, asking the Lord for patience and wisdom. Maybe he should have done that before he leaped into the fray. "What kind of orders are we talking about?"

"The tile for each room in each unit is clearly on the work list. Am I not correct?"

"Uh... I believe so." That was Janessa's department. Maxwell mostly looked for empty holes on the master sheet.

"He put the bathroom tiles for Cottage Four in Cottage Three's bathroom!"

They weren't all the same? Tiles were cheaper by the pallet. Right. He vaguely remembered this discussion from before Heather quit.

Let Janessa not follow in her predecessor's footsteps by leaving him in the lurch. Maxwell needed an experienced interior designer on staff.

"All the tiles are somewhat similar, aren't they?" He could hope.

"Not remotely. The colorways are unique to each cottage. Heather and I specifically chose modern aesthetics to deliver distinctive vibes for each one."

Maxwell massaged his temples. "How far into tiling is he?"

"The master bath is finished, and he's started the hall bath."

Ugh. "Can you just swap the palettes?"

Janessa glared at him. "Only if you want my team to repaint everything and Jordan to tear up and reinstall flooring. He's got a good start in Cottage Three's great room."

Was this really the end of the world if the tile and paint color weren't an absolutely perfect match? Although, like Janessa, he prided himself on attention to detail.

If he'd spent as much time at the project as usual, this would probably not have happened, but he'd been distracted by cascading blond hair and shy blue eyes and hanging around the dining hall.

"Can Steve rip out the tile?"

"He says only with a hammer." Janessa spat out her reply. "And that he can't promise there wouldn't need to be drywall repairs. I bet he'd damage the walls on purpose to spite me."

If she'd come at the guy in this tone of voice, he probably would. "Steve's the best tiler in this part of Montana." Maxwell really, *really* didn't want to have to hunt for another with similar experience.

"What good is that if he's rogue?"

"Rogue?" Maxwell rolled his eyes and shook his head. "It was probably an honest mistake."

"I doubt it. He hates me."

He could sympathize with Steve at the moment. "Look, you're the designer in charge of this project. If you weren't neck-deep in a personal tiff with Steve, what would you recommend? Sounds like we have a few options. One, live with it and carry on." His personal preference.

Janessa huffed.

"Two, he rips out the tile, breaks a few, and we have to order extras out of Chicago and wait a few weeks. So, we'll be held up and in need of minor repairs to the walls. That's if we didn't buy the tail end of that lot of tiles. They may be completely irreplaceable."

She narrowed her gaze at him, her jaw set.

"Three, you repaint, and we swap the palettes as best we can. Paint is relatively cheap and available. Yes, it will set us back several days with the extra time, and I know the labor is on you. Any options I've missed?"

"The one where you fire Steve, or I quit?"

"I do not believe that is an option." He met her gaze as evenly as he could. Waited.

"I hate this!" The words spurted from her mouth as she clenched her fists dramatically. "He's such a jerk."

"Janessa, you need to calm down."

"Is that really all you've got, boss man? *I* need to calm down?"

"First things first. Leadership requires levelheadedness. Personal stuff needs to stay out." A lesson he'd also do well to remember. He hadn't let thoughts of Eryn affect the decisions on the Ladybug Lane project, but he'd definitely been distracted and taken more time away than usual.

He was paying for that right now.

"Tell you what, Janessa. Head into Cottage Five and take an inventory of the paint supplies. How close are we to shifting operations over there?"

"You just don't want me to yell at him some more."

Maxwell stared into her eyes. "Exactly."

She rolled her eyes. "Whatever. The guy's a jerk. He—"

"Janessa. I'll deal with things here."

"Steve's gonna fight you on it. He—"

"I've got it."

She heaved a sigh. "Fine." She flounced down the lane and marched into the fifth cottage.

Maxwell tossed a prayer heavenward. It was time for Steve.

ERYN HADN'T SEEN Maxwell again all day, except for the glimpse she'd had of him at breakfast. She hadn't been ready to talk to him then, and she wasn't ready to talk to him now, but shouldn't he at least be trying to communicate?

Yeah, she'd messed up her own head by welcoming Amelia into it, but Maxwell didn't know that. The question was burning a hole in her mind, though. Would he actually have followed through with his childhood promise if her sister were still alive?

Guaranteed Amelia would have made a push for it.

Maxwell had to be the reason Amelia hadn't ever had a serious boyfriend.

Eryn had spent her entire life in her twin's shadow. Amelia's death should have freed her, but it hadn't. The journals were only part of the problem. Dad didn't know she was reading them, but he still managed to throw Amelia in Eryn's face in front of Maxwell.

The problem was her. She'd been born the smaller twin, the one with a heart defect that required constant monitoring throughout their preschool years. She couldn't help the extra diligence she'd been paid by their parents. Amelia had acted up then to get attention, and she'd never stopped.

But it was on Eryn that she'd allowed Amelia to continue to dominate and bully her for another two decades. Amelia was still controlling her from beyond the grave.

Eryn needed to stop reading the journals, or maybe even get rid of them, but that seemed extreme. Her sister's handwritten log was fascinating... when it wasn't full of spite for Eryn or longing for Maxwell. Then it made Eryn fuming angry, but she couldn't seem to turn away.

If her own twin sister couldn't love her, how could anyone else? Everyone had preferred Amelia. *Maxwell* had.

The flaw was in Eryn, but what could she do about it now? She wasn't assertive. She wasn't suddenly going to grow a backbone and tell people where it was at. That was Amelia's obnoxious way.

She should never have gone to Paisley about Maxwell's birthday, because how could she get out of planning the excursion now, unless they broke up? He'd probably be grateful if she called off their relationship. He would himself later, when he got tired of her needy ways.

When he recalled his promise to Amelia.

Eryn stared at the two books on her nightstand. Her Bible and Amelia's journal. She knew which one she should pick up and read, and it wasn't the diary.

But that's what she reached for.

November 27, 2008

There's nothing to be thankful for without Mom. Groenings invited us over for turkey dinner. Dad says it was nice of them. It wasn't. I hated everything. I hated being polite. I hated Eryn for making a big deal out of Karen's pity, clinging to her and bawling like a baby. Karen is not Mom. But Eryn is such a suck-up she doesn't care. She's been like that forever, hogging all the attention. Just like when she was a bratty kid pretending to be sick.

Eryn stifled a sob. She remembered that day. Remembered how much comfort she'd felt in Mrs. Groening's arms. Dad was barely functioning. Amelia had withdrawn into fury like a caged animal. Eryn had soaked up every bit of the neighbor woman's sympathy. It hadn't been pity. It had been kindness to a young teenage girl who needed someone to love her.

Her hunch about the source of Amelia's hatred had been correct. It was all due to Eryn's heart condition. She hadn't been pretending! What would a baby or a toddler know about that, anyway?

She still needed someone to love her.

Maxwell Sullivan hadn't said the words, but his kind eyes and tender kisses made her think it might become a possibility.

But then he'd discover her fatal flaw. She didn't even know exactly what it was — the heart thing was only Amelia's excuse — but it made people not love her for long. Maxwell would stop caring about her then, and it would break her heart.

She heard the door open downstairs, and she eyed the ladder, not that Dad had ever invaded her loft bedroom.

"Eryn? I'm home."

"Hey, Dad." She kept her voice even.

"Can we talk?"

"I'm pretty tired." Right, it was only 8:30. It wasn't like she was turning out her light any minute soon.

"I hate how I left things last night. I'd like to make things right."

Eryn hated how he'd left things, too, but she didn't want to talk about it. Still, Dad was all she had left, even if he thought the better daughter had died.

"I'll be down in a minute."

"Okay. I'll put on tea."

Tea had been Mom's thing. Eryn doubted Dad had fixed a cup for himself his entire life until Mom had passed away. Now it was his answer to everything.

She scanned the rest of Amelia's entry, but it was more of the same. Poor Amelia. No one understands. My sister is a loser. Yada yada.

If only it didn't hurt so much to know how little Amelia thought of her.

It was self-inflicted pain. Eryn got that, but it seemed she should uncover the depth of the anguish before she could heal from it. Did that make healing the goal? Not likely. She just needed to remember that she wasn't worthy of anything good, and there was no one better than Amelia to keep that in the forefront.

And Dad.

Eryn sighed, tucked the journal into her drawer, and climbed down the ladder.

"I bungled things last night. I'm sorry." Dad's hangdog face might have been funny if it weren't directed at Eryn.

"You brought up good points."

"I did?" He set two teacups on the table.

"If Maxwell wants to run, I'd rather he did it now rather than later."

"It was that talk of his Chicago condo that triggered me. I should have known—"

"No, it's okay. He's too good for the likes of me, so if that conversation convinced him to back off, it's probably for the best."

Dad frowned, obviously turning her words every which way to figure them out.

Good luck with that. Because Eryn couldn't decipher them, either.

"He's not too good for you."

Eryn managed a laugh. "He is. He's rich and self-confident. I'm not in his league." Not like Amelia might have been.

"You're a fine woman, and he'd be lucky to win you."

She shook her head. "Thanks, but I think you're required to say that. We'll see how it plays out, okay?"

"But…" He stared at her a moment longer. "I didn't see him today at all."

"He was at breakfast." A meal Dad took at the farmhouse with Joseph and Marie. "We didn't get a chance to talk, and I haven't seen him since."

"That doesn't sound like him. Are you sure you didn't say something to drive him off?"

"Dad!"

He raised both hands in self-defense. "The young man who was in this kitchen last night wasn't letting go of you."

"That doesn't mean I pushed him away." Although, she kind of had, at breakfast. He'd lingered, and she'd stayed busy, far from the serving counter. She'd wanted to punish him for Amelia's words.

That was so messed up. She knew it, but which way was up?

If he was a pursuer, why wasn't he pursuing?

CHAPTER TWENTY-TWO

I t's not that big a deal." Steve shook with fury. "I quit."

"It is that big of a deal. The correct tile was clearly marked on the work order." Maxwell kept his voice level. "I would rather you didn't leave."

"Right, you won't find another sucker to work up here in these conditions."

As if. "I have connections." Back in Chicago. Getting someone out here might take a bit of juggling, but Maxwell would do it if Steve followed through on his threat. The thing was, the two batches of tile for the two cottages were distinct enough so as not to be interchangeable. He could have had Janessa repaint, but the tile also had to match the cabinetry and countertops and, apparently, the flooring.

"Like I said, I quit. You want that tile removed, do it yourself." Steve glared and pivoted on his booted heel before striding back into the cottage.

The guy might be a talented tiler, but he was full of himself. Janessa teased Maxwell about the same thing. Was he really anything like Steve? He hoped not. Prayed not.

As for the threat that Maxwell needed to do it himself... he could. Back in their early days, he'd been hands-on in every aspect of the flips. He could fix the botched tile job himself if required, but it would cut into his time managing the remainder of the project and certainly cut into his time with Eryn.

He needed a tiler on payroll. They had too many cottages to upgrade, and then there were the repairs in the campground restrooms. As maintenance foreman, Jude had put in a work requisition for upgrades there before leaving for flight school in Chicago. Those needed to be completed before Memorial Day.

Steve exited the cottage, carrying his tile saw.

Drat. Maxwell had left his own tools in Chicago. Hadn't figured he'd need them with a tiler onsite. He'd need to get Grandfather's assistant to ship those out asap. Thankfully, the storage locker had a punch code and didn't require a key. The delay would still set him back all week, but it couldn't be helped.

With a glare Maxwell's direction, Steve stomped back to the cottage and inside, no doubt for the remainder of his tools.

And Maxwell was going to stand right here and make sure the guy didn't take anything extra. He tapped Grandfather's office number.

"Sullivan Enterprises, Tammy speaking."

"Hey, Tammy. This is Maxwell." He outlined what he needed from her and answered her questions. Good thing he was organized enough to know everything was in a couple of clearly marked boxes on the lefthand shelf near the back.

"You've got it, Maxwell. I'll send someone over this afternoon and let you know the shipping info when I've got it."

"Thanks. I owe you one." He tapped to end the call just as Steve jumped in his truck and roared down Ladybug Lane. Then he called Graham and asked for Steve's final compensation to be calculated and mailed, along with his record of employment.

Now, he needed to face the remainder of his team and begin removing the tile. Figuring out how to get a replacement workman out here was going to be a problem for later.

Janessa met him inside the door, hands on her hips. "You fired him?"

"He quit."

She spat some ugly words under her breath. "Of course, he'd quit rather than own up to his mistake. Now what?"

"Now I tear out the tile." He rolled up the sleeves of his flannel shirt.

"You?" Her eyebrows tilted upward.

"Do you see anyone else who can do it? Of course, me." She hadn't been around in the early years, or she wouldn't have implied he didn't know what he was doing.

"Right." She backed away, hands up in surrender. "Just don't make it any worse."

Was he still going to need to sack someone today? He'd been ready to fire Steve if needed, but the decision had been made for him. He was still itching.

"Janessa? I'm the boss. I can do every job a reno like this calls for. I have done them all many times. That includes picking colors and painting walls." Was the threat clear enough?

"Yes, boss." She offered a half-hearted salute and turned to the door. "I'll just be over in Cottage Four if you need me for anything."

"Bring me a plate from lunch when you go down." It was going to be a few hours before he'd worked out his frustrations. Handy that bashing tile was on his agenda.

"Your girlfriend will miss seeing you."

"I'll catch her later. First things first."

That's what Dad would have said, right? Work was the priority over everything else. And look where that had gotten James Sullivan.

Maxwell selected his tools, donned a pair of goggles, laid a protective sheet over the granite counter, and began tapping at the edge of the tile. What a shame, since Steve had done great work. But was it great work if the wrong outcome had been achieved?

What did he have to look forward to at the end of his life? *Well done, good and faithful servant*? Or would it be more along the lines of, *you failed, because you worked really hard with rapt attention to all the wrong details*?

Tap, tap, tap.

But this was his job! With Steve gone, it was up to Maxwell to make sure things got done.

He snorted. Tapped some more. There really was no way to remove these things without breaking them. Yeah, he'd hoped, even though he knew better. So far, only one tile had popped off whole. Probably'd had an air pocket in the mortar.

Broken tiles lay on the counter. Somehow, they looked like his life.

Did they have to? Or could he salvage the tiles of his life without wrecking them? Then again, mosaics were a thing. In life and in renovations, that broken look wasn't the high-end result he was going for, though.

Maxwell became aware of Janessa in the bathroom doorway. She cleared her throat. "Hate to tell you, boss, but they can't get any more of this tile."

He froze, his tool poised on the edge of a tile. "You said they could."

"Yeah, the retailer's inventory said there were enough boxes, but when warehouse went to grab them, they couldn't find them anywhere. They hunted end-over-end and now assume the tiles were sold and someone forgot to update inventory. They sent out a call to other stores in the network, and no one has any."

Looked like they were making a mosaic, after all.

Lemonade out of smashed lemons and all that.

"Maxwell wants a lunch to go." Janessa stared across the counter at Eryn.

Was that smugness? Or was it pity?

Eryn shook it off and lifted her chin. "I'll get it ready." Serving meals was her job, after all. But she hadn't seen him since breakfast yesterday, and she'd tried not to notice him then.

Had Dad scared him off so thoroughly that he'd run blind without even telling her he was through? It didn't make sense. Not the man who'd kissed her sweetly and promised to pursue her through thick and thin.

Whichever this was, he wasn't here. He wasn't pursuing. He was most notably absent.

She poured soup into a snap-lid glass container, fixed a sandwich, and put both into a small, insulated lunch bag, which she passed to Janessa. "Here you go."

"Aren't you going to ask where he is and why he's not here?"

"I figured you'd tell me if he asked you to."

"You two." Janessa rolled her eyes. "We've been having trouble with Steve on the jobsite, and he quit this morning. Maxwell is trying to fix Steve's mistake."

"I see." Of course, it would be work pulling Maxwell's attention. He'd warned her he was a workaholic, but he always came for meals. Didn't he realize she'd wonder about his absence? Wasn't that how he said his parents' marriage had unraveled? His dad spent all his time at work until his mom had enough of being ignored.

Eryn had met Maribel, who seemed nice enough, but she hadn't met James. Both would be visiting over Thanksgiving, along with Maxwell's grandfather and others. It sounded like it should be an interesting weekend… especially if this continued.

"Maxwell doesn't mean to get wrapped up in his work. It just happens."

Was Janessa still here?

Eryn managed a smile. "I understand. You should get that to him while it's still hot. I'm sorry he's having a bad day." No, she didn't comprehend, but she wasn't going to vent her frustration on Maxwell's employee. Or to anyone else, because no one ever understood, anyway.

Amelia's face mocked her.

Eryn banished it.

"Okay, thanks. See you around." Janessa grabbed the cooler and followed Tory and Jordan out of the dining hall.

"Are you okay?" Paisley stood in the spot Janessa had vacated. "Didn't Maxwell show up for lunch today, either?"

Eryn hated pity. "Janessa said one of the workers quit, and he's sorting out the situation."

"Why don't you go up there and talk to him? Remind him there's life beyond the renovation?"

"Are you kidding me?" Eryn pulled back.

"Why not?" Paisley lowered her voice. "You want that guy, you have to go after him. Don't let him shut you out. Prove to him you're a good listener, but more than that? That you're worth spending time with."

"I'm not brave like you." Because wasn't that how Paisley had caught Weston, according to the stories?

"It's not bravery. Not really. It's knowing your own value and holding onto it."

"That's easy, then. I don't have much worth."

"Girl! So not true."

"It is." Tears stung Eryn's eyes. "And I should get back to helping Nadine clean up now."

"You're off in ten minutes?" Paisley stared at her until Eryn finally nodded. "I'm gonna fix myself a cup of tea and sit right over there. And then you are going to get a cup of tea and sit across from me and tell me what's going on. I'm not budging until you do. Got it?"

Eryn's protest died on her lips when she took in the

fierce gleam in Paisley's eyes. She'd never had anyone fight for her like this before. It terrified her... but it was also somewhat gratifying. "Okay."

She turned back into the kitchen, but Nadine waved her away. "Go on early. It's not a problem. There's not much cleanup left to do, anyway."

"Are you sure?"

"Oh, honey, I'm sure. You look like you need a friend, and if Paisley can be that for you, then I'm all for it. She's been so good for my boy."

Those blasted tears were pricking again. "Thanks." She gave Nadine an impulsive hug.

The woman hugged her back. "If you ever need to talk to someone older, I'm right here. And that's not because I rather like your father." Nadine winked.

That was all kinds of awkward. "Okay. Thanks." But what would happen if Dad and Nadine got serious? That would make Nadine her stepmom. Weston and Jude, whom she hadn't met yet, her stepbrothers. Weird.

Paisley had overheard Nadine, because she pointed to two mugs of tea on the table.

Eryn hurried over and yanked the teabag out of one of them. How anyone could drink it as potent as Paisley could was beyond her. She scooped in a little honey and gave it a stir as she sat down.

"Talk to me," Paisley ordered. "Why don't you think you're worthwhile? Because that's not what Jesus says."

"I know. It's just... can you keep this confidential?"

"Of course. I'm almost offended you would think you needed to ask."

"I had a twin sister, Amelia. She..." Eryn gathered a

breath. "She hated me and made my life miserable since we were babies. She was careful that our parents didn't notice, but I'm sure they knew we weren't best friends or anything like that."

Paisley bit her lip but gestured for Eryn to keep going.

"She died in a car crash a couple of years ago now. You'd think I'd feel free, but I've felt so much guilt being the one left behind. Everyone liked her. Me? Not so much."

"I'm sorry. I can't imagine how that all made you feel."

"Everyone assumes we were a tight unit because we were twins. But we were never close, even though I wanted it. She always pushed me away. Belittled me. I could never do anything right."

"And that stuck with you and became how you saw yourself."

Eryn stared into her mug. It was hard to deny.

"You know that's not how God sees you, right?"

"I know," Eryn whispered. "It just seems His voice isn't as loud in my head as Amelia's." And she knew why. "Actually... is there a place I can have a bonfire?"

Paisley blinked. "Pardon me? I missed a transition somewhere."

"I know why her voice is louder, and I have some things I need to burn."

"I'm still not following."

"Her journals." Shame flushed Eryn's cheeks. "I found them just before we moved here, and I've been reading them. I know I shouldn't. First, because they were hers and therefore private. But also, because she kept recording what a loser I am." She wasn't about to mention Amelia's obsession with Maxwell. That wasn't really the point. Not anymore.

"If they have paper or cardboard covers, we can burn them in the fireplace here."

"They do."

"I'll come with you to get them. Let's go right now."

Eryn quaked. What if she wanted to read a few more entries? Maybe she should have sampled a diary from a few years later than junior high.

"Eryn?"

"Okay. Let's do it." She'd still need to figure out what was up with Maxwell, but quieting Amelia's voice would be helpful to her mental health, at least. Even if it didn't change anything else.

CHAPTER TWENTY-THREE

Y ou're a fool, boss. Fire me if you have to."

Maxwell set down his tools, tipped his goggles up, and stared at Janessa. "Pardon me?"

"I don't know why you're avoiding Eryn, but she's miserable."

His ire sputtered. "I'm not avoiding her."

Janessa's head tipped to the side as her eyebrows raised. "Is that how she sees it?"

"Did she ask you where I was? Because you could have told her."

"I did tell her, but Maxwell? She didn't ask. She looked like she expected to be ghosted all along, and now it had come true."

Ouch. Ghosted was a nasty word. But that was basically what he'd done, if only for a day. He braced himself. "I was bound to disappoint her sooner or later."

"Seriously? That's what you've got?"

Maxwell spread his hands. "Whatever I do, it's never enough."

"Hold everything, boss man, and back up a bit. You've accomplished far more in your, what, thirty? years than most anyone I've met."

"Twenty-nine, thanks, anyway." He was willing to own the extra week before his birthday, but an entire year? Nope.

"Even more impressive."

"Get real, Janessa. Thanks for bringing lunch. How's painting going over in Four?"

"I'm giving you free advice." Her jaw took an obstinate edge.

"Which is likely worth exactly what I paid for it." Maxwell pointed at the door.

"Pretend for a minute you're not Maxwell the Great, just an ordinary guy who works too much and is lousy at relationships."

He really ought to fire her. This was more liberty than even Heather had ever taken, and he'd known her for a decade. Janessa? Barely over a year.

On the other hand, she wasn't completely wrong. "Pass me my lunch, and have at it. You've got ten minutes to get this all off your chest, and then you get to never mention it again."

"Gotcha, boss man." She held out the cooler. "It's soup, so you might want to sit at a table somewhere."

The orders never ceased, but he'd granted her ten minutes, and he'd let her use them. Then she could shut it or walk.

He followed her to the small deck, where they'd set up a portable table and a couple of folding chairs. He opened the container and inhaled the aroma of green bean soup, something Aunt Nadine had introduced into his life, along with dozens of other tasty, home cooked foods like he'd never had in his life.

Eryn probably had made the soup. She may even have made the sourdough bread cradling ham salad between the slices.

She'd never been far from Kansas but had uprooted her entire life, everything she'd ever known, to follow where Maxwell had beckoned. Sure, she'd come with her dad, but this might as well have been a foreign land to both of them.

And now he was too wrapped up in work even to set her mind at rest.

But hadn't he proved to himself that he was just like his father? And that meant work first, second, and third. Relationships were down in fourth place, if even there.

"Boss?"

He focused on Janessa as he took a bite of the sandwich then motioned her to talk.

"There's more to life than work."

For some people, maybe. He chewed. She had ten minutes — nine, now — and she might as well spend them all talking.

"I hear you're a Christian. I've never heard you cuss, and you go to church."

That was her definition of Christianity? Ugh. He'd definitely failed.

"I'm no expert, but doesn't that mean you answer to a higher power than the almighty dollar?" Janessa held both hands as though in defense. "I know your family is filthy rich, and I get that we need money to make the world go 'round, but it's not God. Or it shouldn't be."

Against his better judgment, he was with her so far. He took a bite of soup. Waited.

"You've watched the Christmas Carol movie or read the book, right?"

He nodded. An animated version when he was a kid… and he saw where she was going with this. Eight minutes.

"So old Ebenezer Scrooge pushed everyone aside in order to get rich—"

Maxwell had had enough. "Hold it right there. I am not like him."

"He pushed everyone aside in order to get rich, but he was alone and grouchy. Money can't keep you warm. Money can't laugh with you. Money can't buy sunsets or sweetgrass wafting on a summer breeze or an ocean lapping at the shore. It can't buy the things that really matter."

"I have a job to do." And he didn't care about money. Not that much. It was approval he craved.

She scoffed lightly and shook her head. "Your grandfather will fire you if the project is set back by a few days? Not likely. I'm willing to bet you don't have to prove anything to him. He knows you're conscientious. And that, by the way, is not the same thing as being a workaholic."

She was right that neither Grandfather nor Tate would fire him. And if they did, Maxwell could go back to running his own business his own way. But he also didn't have to prove anything to God, so who was he trying to impress?

Himself? The people around him? What really drove him? He didn't even know.

Yes, he did. Dad. No matter how hard he worked, James

Sullivan found ways to make him feel inept. At least if he poured everything into work, he could look better to Dad than Bryce.

Bingo.

Appearing better than his brother in his father's eyes drove him. Wasn't that pathetic? Bryce was a grown man of thirty. He made his own choices. Maxwell wasn't responsible for him, and one-up-man-ship wasn't a good look on anyone.

"Just think about what you're doing to Eryn as well as to yourself. I think she could be really great for you, but relationships don't happen by accident. They take time and attention."

Maxwell's eyebrows tilted up as he studied Janessa. Where was this advice coming from? It sounded personal.

Janessa pulled to her feet. "Yeah, I've been there. I'll leave you to it."

He glanced at his watch. "You've got three more minutes. Why not give me the other barrel?'

She laughed mirthlessly. "There is no other barrel, boss man. It was all in that first one. Don't be an Ebenezer Scrooge and wake up a bitter old man, surrounded by gold coins but with no one to love. That's the whole sermon." She turned away.

"Gold coins? I wish!" Maxwell tried for a jovial tone.

Janessa pointed a finger at him. "That there is exactly what I'm talking about."

"It was a joke," he mumbled.

The door into the cottage closed behind her.

Had it been a joke, or did he believe that more money made things better? He had enough for a comfortable lifestyle for the rest of his life already. Maybe not if he found himself cut off from the Sullivan fortune, but even so, he was unlikely to ever be destitute.

Keith Ralston had needed to sell the farm that had been in his family for generations because of overwhelming debt. His house had once been grand, or at least, fairly nice, but it had fallen into disrepair over decades of neglect. Not likely because Keith had preferred to spend his money on other things, but because there hadn't been enough to go around.

Eryn hadn't lived with her dad from inertia, but because of the cost of living. Her clothes weren't up to date in fashion. Not that Maxwell cared, but most women he knew did. Men's fashion was more forgiving, at least in the construction world where he dabbled.

He came from a world of have. She came from a world of have not. And now he'd made her feel that she was less than, as well.

Great. He needed to think and pray on that while he chipped out more tile.

Biting her lip, Eryn opened her backpack in the lodge's great room. She'd left Paisley downstairs at the duplex and packed the journals herself, steeling herself against their siren call. Just one more entry couldn't hurt, right?

Oh, but it could. She knew that now.

Paisley knelt in front of the fireplace and nudged the mesh screen aside before beckoning Eryn beside her.

Eryn lowered herself to a cushion on the hearth and

took a deep breath. There was still time to gather the books and run. Keep those reminders — those hurts — close to her chest.

"There's a lot to be said about getting rid of bad memories," Paisley mused, watching the flames dance. "I've had a bit of practice."

"You have?"

"My mom's a mess. She was a drug addict for years, then came clean, then relapsed in June. I don't have a lot of good memories from my childhood."

Amelia notwithstanding, Eryn did have some.

"I met my father for the first time in June," Paisley went on. "He's scum. I never want to see him again."

Eryn winced. "I'm sorry." At least her own dad was an upstanding man.

"My sisters…" Paisley took a deep breath. "They try, I guess. Kait looks after Mom, but she's bitter. Like you, I have a sister named Amelia. She's the oldest, and she ditched the rest of us as soon as she could. She's back east somewhere. Last I heard, she was nearly through med school on scholarships. I ran away, too, but with less to show for it. I didn't have Amelia's focus. I worked seasonal jobs for years: ski lodges in winter, resorts like Sweet River in summer."

"I never guessed." Eryn had been focused inwardly, not looking out to see who else might be hurting, and why. What kind of friend did that make her? A lousy, selfish one.

Paisley shrugged. "I cover it up well, I suppose. But running from the past doesn't change it, and it doesn't allow healing." She looked at Eryn. "Dwelling in it doesn't, either."

"You're right." Eryn pulled the top journal out. 2008. She'd read the whole thing. "Do I need to tear it up, or will it burn okay whole?"

"Looks easy to tear, and it might be therapeutic."

Eryn snorted under her breath. Her friend had no idea. Or maybe she did. She grasped the notebook, twisted it, and ripped it in half. Then she fed the pieces to the blaze, watching as the flames danced on the paper before blackening it. Poof. The first handful was gone.

Panic threatened to engulf her the same way the flames engulfed the next bundle of paper. But no, this was the right thing to do. She'd known it all along, but today was the first time she'd been brave enough to face the challenge.

2010 was half read, and now she would never finish. It likely held more of the same, and she didn't need to wallow in it. It was the past. Amelia was dead, and with these journals burned, her power to hurt Eryn would also disappear.

Okay, not completely, because short of a major bout of amnesia, memories would remain. But maybe with practice, she could keep them from affecting every minute of every day.

Wow, she couldn't believe she'd been a slave to these stupid diaries for nearly two months. Burning the pages felt like unlocking shackles from around her ankles. Not that prisoners had a choice, but Eryn did, and she was taking it.

Freedom.

Paisley's quiet voice seeped into her mind. "Therefore, if anyone is in Christ, the new creation has come: the old has gone, the new is here!"

Eryn looked at her.

"Second Corinthians 5:17. It's been both a challenge and a comfort to me."

Eryn fed another wad of paper into the fire.

"Ooh, a book burning! What's the occasion?" Bryce's taunting voice came from behind them. "I prefer to read banned books rather than burn them."

Eryn's heart chilled to ice, and she clutched the backpack to her chest. "Get out of here."

He laughed. "Whatcha hiding? Is it something my little brother should know? I always have his best interests at heart, as I'm sure you know."

"Get lost, Bryce." Paisley sounded bored. "This is none of your business. Don't you have someplace you need to be?"

He dropped into an easy chair nearby. "Nope. I came in to enjoy the fire."

Could Eryn keep going with him watching? It would be so much easier to take her backpack back to the duplex and try again later. Or maybe just keep the journals. She didn't have to read them. No one was forcing her to.

No. She'd come this far. She tore the next one in half and tossed it into the blaze. Once it was mostly consumed, she did it again. Then again.

"Old love letters? I bet Maxie would love to read those."

"None of your business, Bryce," Paisley warned.

Eryn didn't need to worry about Bryce. Paisley would take care of him if he tried to snatch the booklets from her. She had only one job: burn the books. Today. Right now.

2014. They were through high school now. Was Amelia

still obsessed with Maxwell? Was she remembering their marriage pact and dreaming about it?

Eryn fumbled the next diary, and it dropped open. She clenched her eyes shut as she closed it then tore it. She needed her eyes open to feed the fire, though.

This was getting easier, year by year. With every destroyed diary, the backpack in her lap grew lighter. Her heart grew lighter.

Eryn was unlikely to conjure up memories of her twin's devotion and love for her, but they weren't in those books, anyway.

They might be.

No. They weren't.

Eryn tossed the last three into the fire without ripping them first. She needed them gone. Absolutely, irrevocably gone.

Now, they were.

The panic subsided, but where had the tears come from? "I'm sorry, Amelia," she whispered. "I forgive you."

Bryce snorted and stalked from the room, his boot heels clacking across the floor until the lodge doors closed behind him.

She'd survived burning the journals while Bryce watched.

And she had a new girlfriend — Paisley Teele — who had her back like no one ever had before. She reached to hug her. "Thank you."

CHAPTER TWENTY-FOUR

S he wasn't at the lodge. She wasn't at the duplex. Where could she be? The stable? Maxwell snapped his fingers. That was likely.

Yeah, he could text or phone her, but the way things were between them, she might not answer, and that was unacceptable.

He pointed his truck up Pegasus Lane and pulled to a stop beside the stable doors. The round pen was empty. No Echo. No Eryn. He jumped out of his truck and strode to the doors.

Inside the horse barn, he paused a moment for his eyes to adjust to the dimmer light. Listened, but the only sounds that came to his ears were swishing tails and shifting feet.

He made his way toward Echo's stall and the makeshift office nook, then stopped in his tracks when he caught sight of Eryn with her arms wrapped around the filly's neck, her long blond hair curtaining her face.

Was that a sniffle? Man, she was crying.

A knife twisted in Maxwell's gut. Janessa had been

right. He'd been too focused on his own stuff to think about how he was affecting Eryn. Yeah, he'd been a little hurt by her dad's interrogation and Eryn seemingly ignoring him at breakfast yesterday, but had his response been any better?

No. No, it had not.

"Eryn?" He kept his voice soft so as not to startle her.

Her head whipped around, her eyes large. "Maxwell?"

"I thought I might find you here. Do you have a few minutes?"

She closed her eyes and squeezed Echo's neck as though she were gathering strength. Finally, she managed, "Okay," as though she'd accepted being led to the gallows.

Eryn was killing him. "Hey. Come here." He held his arms out to her.

She bit her lip and let go of the filly but kept her distance. "Just tell me what you need to say."

Did she think he'd changed his mind about their relationship? Far from it. He tugged one of her hands free and pulled her gently down the alleyway and out the doors into the early November sunshine. A set of bleachers nearby offered seating for the gymkhanas Paisley and Weston arranged for kids to test their horsemanship prowess.

Still holding Eryn's hand, Maxwell settled on the second level. She pulled free and sat down nearby. But not close. He turned to study her.

She stared at the fingers twisting in her lap and audibly gulped.

"Eryn, I treated you badly. I'm sorry."

She glanced his way but didn't quite meet his gaze.

"Your dad's not completely wrong."

Now she seemed to cower. Great, would he ever get this right? "Eryn? I'm not sure I'm good enough for you, but I promise that you're not a game to me. I'm serious about my attraction to you, but I feel like I'm receiving mixed signals from you." He scrubbed his hands through his hair. "And then I sent them back by disappearing. Or maybe they didn't seem mixed. Maybe they felt like full-on rejection. I want to tell you why, but I'm afraid it will sound like excuses, not reasons. And there's no excuse good enough to ignore you, and I'm sorry."

"*You're* apologizing to *me?*"

"Yes? I wronged you. I got so involved solving a problem at the cottages — Steve made a huge error on a tile job, then we had words and he quit, then I tried to fix it all — I told myself you didn't want to talk to me because of your dad and because I couldn't catch your eye at breakfast yesterday, and... Eryn?"

She cradled her face in her hands while her shoulders quaked.

He'd made her cry. Maxwell scooted closer and slipped his arm around her shoulder. "Hey, sweetie. I'm sorry."

Now she was sobbing in earnest.

Maxwell had no sisters, and if his mother ever cried, it was far from her sons' sight. What should he say? He was out of his league. He rubbed his palm over her upper arm. *God? I could use some help here...*

"I'm sorry, too," she got out between sobs.

"You haven't done anything wrong, sweetie. It was on me."

Eryn shook her head. "I've done plenty wrong."

When she was quiet too long, he murmured, "Haven't we all? That's why Jesus came."

"I've been jealous of Amelia my entire life. Everyone liked her. No one even n-n-noticed me."

Maxwell's memories mocked his rebuttal before he uttered it. Eryn was right. He barely remembered her as more than a shadowy figure from his childhood. Like a diva, Amelia had commanded center stage.

"I only wanted to be her friend. Everyone talks about the twin bond, but we never had that. She always hated me."

Hated was a strong word, but Maxwell kept his mouth zipped. Eryn was talking, and this was what she believed, and he needed to hear her out, even though the topic wasn't quite what he'd expected. He kept stroking her upper arm. Waited.

"She had a thing for you."

Maxwell winced, but it was undeniable.

Eryn shot a barely perceptible glance his way. "She got you to promise to marry her if you were both old and unattached."

He pulled away and stared at Eryn. "Wait. What?"

"She wrote it in her journal. It was after Mom's funeral."

How did he not recall this? He remembered the funeral. Remembered the luncheon. Remembered feeling guilty that while he was celebrating a birthday, others mourned a life cut short.

"You don't remember?" Eryn asked plaintively.

Maxwell shook his head. "She was crying." What else?

"You hugged her."

"I did? You saw that?"

Eryn's face flushed and she looked down. "She wrote it in her journal."

Just a sec. That was the second time she'd said that. "She kept a journal?" And Eryn had read it?

"This is the part where I'm sorry, okay?"

He nodded slowly.

"She had a notebook for every year from seventh grade on. I found them when Dad and I cleared out her room when we... lost the farm. Just before we moved here."

Eryn had read her sister's private words. He could see the temptation would have been great. Would he have succumbed? He had no clue, but he hoped not. Thankfully, his brothers weren't likely to be journal-keepers, and he'd never discover how he'd react.

"I shouldn't have read any of it. I know that. I knew Amelia... hated me." Her voice broke again.

Maxwell's hand resumed stroking her arm. He could offer that much support, at least, though it didn't seem like much.

"And she did hate me. The sentiment was clear in nearly every entry."

"How could you keep absorbing that?"

"You mean in life, or in the diaries?"

"Either." He shook his head. "Both."

"In life, because it was my reality. I didn't know anything else. In her journals? That's harder to answer."

Maxwell waited.

"Partly..." She gave a shuddering sob. "I saw you through her eyes. She adored you."

"Eryn?" When she didn't meet his gaze, he turned her

face toward his with a gentle touch to her chin. "She's not here. Don't let her be here, between us."

"I know." She gulped. "But you always keep your promises. You told me so."

She was right. He had said that... but he didn't remember anything about marrying Amelia. Could anyone have held him to that? He'd been a kid! "She's dead, Eryn." He gentled his voice as best he could considering the turmoil inside him.

"She would have pressured you to follow through."

"She wouldn't have succeeded."

"But... promises."

"Occasionally, people make vows they shouldn't, without all the facts. Sometimes people make ones they fully intend to keep, but things happen to intervene." Maxwell gave a mirthless laugh. "Like my parents' marriage. If you look at their wedding pictures, they were all eyes for each other. Big smiles. I'm pretty sure my dad didn't intend to break his promise to love and cherish her."

"I get that."

Did she? He caressed her jaw while his other hand tugged her closer to remove the gap between them. "We're human. Only God is perfect at it, but that doesn't let us off the hook. We still need to make promises carefully then do everything within our power to fulfill them. But we can't control everything, and we can't control someone else."

Now her eyes searched his. "You're right. I maybe read too much into that."

"I want to make promises to you, Eryn. I think... no, I know I love you. But I don't want to make them until I'm really, really sure. Until *you* are really, really sure."

"You… love me?"

He hugged her. "I do, but I don't want to scare you."

Eryn shook her head. "You're not scaring me, because I maybe love you, too. But you're right about making sure." She took a deep breath. "I burned Amelia's journals in the lodge fireplace after lunch. Paisley stayed with me and encouraged me."

Bless Paisley. Relief swept through Maxwell. He'd been trying to figure out how to broach the subject.

"She told me that reading them was like going up to Amelia every day and asking her to remind me why I was unworthy of love. Why she hated me and why everyone else should, too."

"Oh, sweetie." Maxwell pressed a kiss to Eryn's temple. "I wish I could challenge your memory and tell you it couldn't have been that bad, but I have no evidence to support it. How did your parents respond?"

"I don't think they realized. They knew we weren't close, but Amelia kept the nastiness private. She knew I wouldn't tell, and she was right."

And then she'd harbored the hurt closer by reliving it all through the entries. Maxwell's heart ached for her. It wasn't possible to get through life unscathed, but she'd made it even harder for herself than it needed to be.

"Then there was Dave Gerbrandt. I don't know if you remember him." Her voice was tiny but determined, as though she knew if she didn't blurt everything right now, she might never find the courage again.

Dave. Dave. Dave? "Vaguely. He wasn't at the reunion, I don't think?"

"He was a class ahead of us in school. A few years ago, he began coming around, asking me out."

News to Maxwell, but he stuffed the jealousy deep. That had been then. Obviously, nothing had come of it.

"We dated a few weeks, and I was so happy. Finally, someone saw me for me, you know?"

This didn't have a happy ending. Maxwell knew it, but a happy ending then would have changed everything for him now.

"As soon as Amelia figured out I had a boyfriend, she turned her charm on him, and in the blink of an eye, the two of them were dating. That's what Dave had wanted all along. He'd only used me to get to my sister, and it worked. I fell for it."

Maxwell winced. "That must have hurt."

"It killed me. They didn't last long. Amelia wasn't into commitment." Eryn glanced at him. "Maybe she was holding out for you to keep your promise."

Was that going to keep coming up between them?

He turned on the bleacher seat and took her face between both his palms. "Eryn? Is there anything else you need to tell me about your twin sister? If not, then I'm done with her. I don't want her to have any power over you and me. She's not here. I'm sorry she died and left your relationship unresolved, but I can't change that. All I can do is tell you that you are absolutely worthy of being loved for who you are."

Her lips trembled. "That's what Paisley said, too."

Maxwell owed Paisley big time. "But even if it turns out that you and I decide to part ways, that wouldn't change your worth." He brushed his lips over her forehead. "Don't get me wrong. I'm not planning to go anywhere, but the fact doesn't change. You are worthy in God's sight. It is God who gives you meaning. He offered you to be part of His family."

"So many times in the past couple of months I chose to read Amelia's mean, dismissive words at night instead of God's words of love and assurance. That ends today." She sniffled. "We are what we read, after all. If all we take in is trash, it can't make us better people."

"That's true. I haven't been reading anyone's journals, but I've still neglected my quiet time more often than I'd prefer to admit. But we're being honest here, so… there's that. I tell myself I don't have time, that whatever is waiting for me at work can't wait another fifteen minutes." Maxwell shook his head. "And that's a lie, too. Nothing should be more important to me than starting out my day in God's word. Smashing tile can wait a bit."

"I thought you had it all together."

"I don't." He waited until she lifted her blue eyes to meet his. Now there was hope — cleansing, maybe — in her gaze. "Are we okay?"

Eryn nodded, and Maxwell dipped his face to hers until their lips met.

He caressed her lips with his own, giving the love he couldn't quite put into words yet, receiving hers.

Only the stomp of the filly's hoof and her whinny brought him back to the present.

CHAPTER TWENTY-FIVE

Eryn looked around the decorated lodge with its streamers, the snack and s'more table, the stack of firewood. Everything was ready. She could only hope Maxwell would be as thrilled with the revised birthday party plan as he'd seemed to be about the trail ride.

Weather. As hard as it was to foresee in Kansas, apparently it was even harder in the mountains. Storms came up out of seemingly thin air. Normal, they said.

Nothing about Montana was normal. Not the mountains. Not the ranch. Not the sweet little town of Jewel Lake. Not her dad contentedly dating. Not the seeds of hope and love rooting inside her as she and Maxwell grew closer every day. Not the joy she was starting to find in the daily Bible reading plan she and Maxwell had committed to doing together yet apart.

"There!" Paisley dusted her hands together as she looked around the lodge with a satisfied smile. "Party 101!"

"It looks great." Eryn offered her friend a shy smile. "I couldn't have pulled this off without you."

"You're right about that." Paisley laughed. "No one but me knows all the places the resort's party inventory is stashed. And no one has as many activity boards on Pinterest as I do to pull ideas from."

Eryn could learn a little self-confidence from her friend, but she didn't want to turn into her. Being Paisley must be exhausting.

Weston came in with one more armload of firewood and added it to the reserves on the hearth. "Brr. The wind is really picking up out there."

"You haven't met wind until you've spent a few weeks in Kansas."

He shook his head. "Remind me never to go there. I'm a Montana boy, through and through."

Paisley nestled against her fiancé. "Sometime, we should go to their Easter passion play, though. It sounds impressive."

"Maybe." He kissed her hair. "Is it that great, Eryn?"

"It is. It's probably the only thing about Gilead that I'll miss." Though she should let Letty and Joannie know she'd landed on her feet. If she had, at least. No, that was the old Eryn talking. She *knew* she was in a better place mentally as well as physically, and Paisley had a lot to do with that. As did Maxwell.

Boots stomped on the front deck, and the door opened, bringing with it a swirl of snowy wind as well as several bundled-up figures. Maxwell's gaze came straight to Eryn, and his smile was visible in his eyes even before he unwound his scarf.

Cadence and Kaci came in, laughing and talking, while Bryce removed his boots and set them in the tray, Graham right behind him. Maxwell had elected not to invite his work crew to this more intimate gathering.

Eryn wasn't so sure about Bryce, either. Now he took Kaci's coat and hung it. She thanked him but didn't give him the adoring look he was probably angling for. Eryn kind of wished they hadn't had to invite Bryce, but it would have been rude, and they were trying to be better. Something was certainly going on in Maxwell's middle brother to make him so abrasive.

"Are Tate and Stephanie coming?" Maxwell crossed the space to the fireplace and scooped Eryn into a bone-crushing hug.

"Yes. My dad and Nadine headed to their house to watch the boys about ten minutes ago, so they should be here soon."

He looked into her eyes. "You okay with them dating?"

"Yeah." She chuckled. "It's weird, but Dad's so happy. I hadn't realized what a huge strain he was under in Kansas after Mom's death and then Amelia's and all the medical bills and… everything. With all that weight off his back, plus a new love, he's doing so well I hardly recognize him some days. He even whistles! He hasn't done that in years."

Maxwell's eyes crinkled with his grin. "I'm glad. I'd hate for him to be unhappy when you and I are on the same page. We are, right?"

"You know it." She stretched to give him a quick kiss.

Bryce made a gagging sound.

Maxwell didn't turn around. "And you wonder why no good woman will have you, bro?"

"Who wants a *good* woman?"

"Me." Maxwell gazed into Eryn's eyes. "I want a good woman, and I've found her."

"Ain't that grand," Bryce muttered.

Paisley clapped her hands. "Okay, we've got some games to get our evening started while we wait for Stephanie and Tate. Charades, guys against girls."

A collective groan went up.

"You'll love it! You know you will."

"But do I know that?" Maxwell whispered into Eryn's ear. "I thought we were going to dance the night away, and I could just hold you close for hours and hours."

Eryn shivered with anticipation. "It's coming, but I let Paisley run with the program, so we're at her mercy."

"Charades, huh. Can't remember when... or even if... I've done that before."

"Me, either," she giggled.

"Hey, birthday boy. You're up first. Get over here."

"You heard the party boss," Weston drawled. "Don't make her come after you."

"Yeah, Maxie," Bryce snarked.

Maxwell turned his back to the group and gave Eryn a slow kiss until her knees melted. Then he grinned, pecked her nose, and turned toward the others. "You were saying?"

The lodge door opened, and Stephanie and Tate stomped in. "We're here. Let the party begin!" Stephanie called.

"It already did." Bryce slumped into one of the easy chairs. "You're late."

"We had to make sure our babysitters weren't going to be so busy kissing they'd ignore Jamie. Not that he allows himself to be ignored." Stephanie glanced between Weston and Eryn. "Maybe you didn't want to know that about your parents."

"More power to them." Weston shook his head, but he had a small smirk.

"What he said." Eryn exchanged a nod with him.

Paisley waved her arms. "Get your coats off, and join our charades game. Guys against girls, and Maxwell was just ready to get us started."

"No snacks?" Tate sent a hopeful look toward the kitchen.

"Like you haven't eaten this week. Games first. Honestly, you guys are more trouble than a dozen tweenagers."

Eryn leaned against Maxwell while they waited. Paisley might think this group was rebellious, but Eryn was in seventh heaven. This was the first time she'd helped plan a party of peers, let alone one to honor her boyfriend. These were all her friends now, too.

Even Bryce?

She could reserve judgment on him. Probably.

"Finally." Maxwell held Eryn close in the dim lantern light as the music swirled around them. "This was the part of my party I was looking forward to."

She smiled up at him, and he thought his heart would explode.

"May I have this dance?"

Who was Bryce talking to? Not Eryn, hopefully.

Maxwell turned his girl enough to see Bryce with his hand out to Kaci.

"Looks like we're the only unattached ones here," Bryce said.

She huffed. "I suppose, but don't let it go to your head."

"I'm a good dancer," he protested.

"You'd better be, because if you tread on my toes, that's the end of it."

"Scout's honor."

Maxwell stifled a laugh. As if the Sullivan boys had been in Scouts. His father had seen no use in the kind of preparedness that particular movement taught, and Maxwell hadn't cared enough to fight him. Take away his chess club, and he might have protested.

A half hour later, they broke for refreshments… again. Eryn left for the restroom, leaving Maxwell standing in the great room with a plate of canapés.

"Nice party, Maxie."

He turned to Bryce. Would it really have been insufferably rude not to invite this brother? "All Paisley and Eryn's doing."

"Must be nice to have a girlfriend."

"You've had dozens."

Bryce shrugged. "Whatever."

"You said you didn't want a *good* woman, but that's the only kind worth building a life with."

"You're going to propose to her?" Bryce rolled his eyes.

"Not today or anytime soon, but yeah, that's where we're headed." Warmth settled in Maxwell's soul. "She's worth every bit of it."

"I hear good women want good men, so yay for you, I guess."

"No one is good, bro. The Bible—"

Bryce held up his hand. "Don't even."

"Sorry, can't help it. The Bible says there is no one good, no, not one. That's why Jesus came. You heard it growing up in Sunday school, same as me."

"But you believed it."

Maxwell studied his brother. "I can't make sense of the universe, of nature, of people, of hopes and dreams and satisfaction without that faith."

"Must be nice to feel so confident. About anything at all."

"You can, too."

Bryce shook his head. "I don't think so. No one cares."

"I care."

"Yeah, don't spout that at me, Maxie. If there's a God, He's not interested in the likes of me."

"That's where you're wrong. You are exactly who God is interested in. You remember the parable Jesus told about leaving the 99 sheep to rescue the one who needed it most?"

Bryce shook his head. "You're in deep."

Maxwell looked past his brother to see that others were watching them but giving them space. Eryn and the other women were adding refreshments to the table, not that it had been sparse. "Bryce? I haven't been a very good brother to you. Sorry about that. But it's not because I don't care. Everyone needs a friend." Just look how Eryn had blossomed over the past couple of months. It hadn't only been

Maxwell. It had been Paisley and Cadence and Kaci and the others, too. Aunt Nadine.

"The thing is…" Bryce raised an eyebrow at Maxwell. "It's kind of too late."

"Dude. You're 30. Grandfather is 82 and look at him. He'll be out next week for Thanksgiving, and want to make a bet he brings Eleanor for dinner? He's doing what he can to make amends for the mistakes he made when he was young. There's no moratorium on fixing things."

Bryce snorted. "Where there's life, there's hope?"

"You've got it."

"I'm pretty sure that's not how it works, but thanks, I guess."

"What's your biggest regret?" Since everyone was still giving them space, Maxwell might as well go for it.

"You'd never understand." Bryce lifted his glass. "And also, why are we drinking pop like we're underage?"

"I happen to want my faculties about me."

"Figures." Bryce downed the pop in one gulp. "I might call the evening early."

"I thought you brought your sleeping bag for the sleepover."

Bryce shook his head. "Still with the juvenile party. I doubt it. My bed's more comfortable."

"We didn't get to do stuff like this when we were kids." Both parents had made sure their boys knew they were a cut above the rest of Gilead. "I'm kind of enjoying it now."

Bryce huffed.

"Stick around, bro. Kaci danced with you, right?"

"She did, but she made sure I remembered she hates my

guts even while we danced. I've never had so much fun in my life."

"Remember how Weston was the grumpy one when we first met him?"

"Before he turned into a mushy mess. Yeah?"

"He was lonely and putting up a facade so people wouldn't realize he cared. That's what you're doing, bro."

"Nope."

Maxwell smacked his brother's shoulder. "You can deny all you want, but you're more transparent than you think. You care, Bryce. And it's not too late to turn around. I'm not talking about Kaci, though who knows? I'm talking about whatever's going on inside you that makes you keep everyone at arm's length."

"Wow, Maxie, I didn't know you cared." Bryce set his plate and cup on the table, strode to the door, shrugged on his jacket, and headed out.

Not what Maxwell had expected.

No, he hadn't expected Bryce to show up at all, let alone allow Maxwell to catch any glimpses of what was going on inside him. Guilt stabbed him. Had he been praying for his brother? Nope. He hadn't. It didn't matter that it was only recently he'd started praying systematically at all. His brother should have been on the list. He would be now.

"You okay?" Eryn asked softly as she slipped an arm around his waist.

"Yeah, I am." Maxwell stared pensively at the door before dropping a kiss to Eryn's temple. "I just realized how much I need to pray for my brother. He's not a very happy guy for all he tries to portray a devil-may-care attitude."

"I've been praying for him."

"You have? You're better at this stuff than I am."

"Who is it who told me everything in life isn't a competition?" She tapped her chin thoughtfully.

He grabbed her finger and kissed it. "Okay, okay. You win." Then he laughed. "I didn't mean it that way."

"Dance with me?" Eryn sounded wistful.

"I'd love to." How did the old Anne Murray song go? *Could I have this dance for the rest of my life...*

He couldn't ask Eryn that yet, but it was coming. Tonight, holding her close before letting her go was enough. Memories were being made with his girlfriend, his brothers and cousins and friends.

Maxwell wasn't generally a patient sort of guy, but Eryn? She was worth every slow step of the dance.

CHAPTER TWENTY-SIX

axwell leaned back in his chair and surveyed the group around the dinner table. Paisley had directed the creation of one long table for Thanksgiving dinner then, with Kaci's help, decorated it and the entire main floor of the lodge with cozy fall themes. Nadine and Eryn had created an amazing feast, and Keith Ralston had carved the turkey.

Dad certainly didn't know how, since the caterers had always done that back when Maxwell was a kid and their family still gathered.

Maxwell's gaze lingered on Grandfather, who leaned toward Eleanor as though listening intently to whatever she was saying. They'd reconnected a year and a half ago. Was anything going to come out of that reunion besides friendship? Only time would tell, but Grandfather was already 82! This was the man who'd quipped he was too old to buy his bananas green. He shouldn't let grass grow beneath his feet if he planned to reignite an old flame. Or was it Eleanor who was dragging her heels? Maybe it was her son Reggie, whom she lived with. He seemed to have strong opinions.

What about Maxwell's parents? Mom had frostily informed Dad she'd fly commercial so he wouldn't have to bother going out of his way to pick her up for Thanksgiving and the board meetings they'd all be having at Sweet River tomorrow. Dad had told her not to be ridiculous; he knew his place and was flying to Montana via Gilead. Now, Mom seemed excessively bright and cheery and just as focused on ignoring her ex as she'd ever been.

Maybe it was Maxwell's imagination. Maybe he was so in love with Eryn that he was seeing heart-filled, starry eyes everywhere. Or maybe his parents didn't hate each other as much as he'd always thought.

Add them to your prayer list.

Yes, God.

Uncle Theodore and Aunt Bridget were in attendance. They'd finally forgiven Graham for marrying Cadence back in September.

Jude was home on break from his pilot studies in Chicago, laughing easily and looking far more self-assured than he ever had before. Being away had been good for him.

And it wasn't likely Maxwell's imagination that Jude's gaze kept straying to Kaci's. It seemed some kind of magic that she could stare at him for half the time while he stared at her the other half, and they rarely caught each other in the act. When were they going to admit their attraction? There had to be something going on. Maxwell wasn't wet behind the ears or oblivious. Not anymore.

Grandfather cleared his throat. "As is our custom, I'd

like us to go around the table and tell everyone what we are most thankful for." He looked at each of them, the pause lengthy for the number of people. "Let's keep it to things not romance."

Groans and laughter surrounded the table.

Maxwell's family. Three years ago, it had all been about business, but now they were friends, too.

"I'll start," Grandfather went on. "I'm thankful to have found my daughter and her mother."

"No romance, you said!" Tate called out.

Everyone laughed.

Grandfather smiled at Eleanor, who looked down. Was that a flush on her cheeks?

"Not talking about romance, boy," the old man said. "Reconnecting with the past, that's all."

Eleanor looked around the table. "I'm thankful my daughter is happy and at peace."

More chuckles.

"I'm thankful for my newest kitchen helper," Nadine said.

"You mean Eryn... or her father?" Weston drawled.

His mother's eyes twinkled. "You may take that however you like, but rules are rules."

Keith's gaze met Maxwell's across the table. "I'm thankful Maxwell offered me a job here at Sweet River. That relocation changed my life and my daughter's life in the best of possible ways."

Everyone was hedging around the romance angle, causing laughter.

"I feel like I've missed a lot around here." Jude glanced around. "While I'm thankful to be fulfilling my dream of getting my pilot's license, I'll be glad to move back to the ranch come springtime."

The circuit continued until it was Eryn's turn. Maxwell squeezed her hand.

"I'm thankful that God always keeps His promises," she said quietly. "Even when we aren't worthy of that, He is always faithful."

Maxwell's heart nearly burst with pride. "I'm thankful for the same thing, but also for the power of prayer. I've been learning to turn things over to God, and it's rewarding."

Bryce huffed under his breath, and Maxwell turned to him. "Your turn, bro."

"What's there to be thankful for?" Bryce muttered.

Silence.

"Okay, fine. I'm thankful for a good life in the Sullivan family." He motioned to Mom on his other side.

Not exactly what Grandfather had been going for. Had Maxwell come across as too pious? But if he couldn't place thankfulness for Eryn at the top of his verbal list, his deeper walk with God was truly the best thing. It took supremacy, either way.

If only Bryce would get over whatever his hang-up was. He'd never taken life seriously, but his moods had grown darker in the past couple of years. Maxwell purposed to pray for his brother even more… and to watch for any opportunities to listen.

When the circuit was complete, Keith cleared his throat and rose to his feet. "I've got an announcement."

Eryn's fingers tightened around Maxwell's, and a quick glance showed her smiling at her father.

Keith nodded at Grandfather at the head of the table. "I wasn't allowed to be thankful for romance a few minutes ago, but everyone has had their say, right? Now, I'd like you all to know that I asked Nadine to marry me, and she said yes!"

"Congratulations!" Maxwell called out, echoed by several others.

"We're planning a small New Year's Eve wedding—"

"I'm on it!" Paisley yelled then quieted. "I mean, if you want me to be."

Laughter burst around the table.

Keith grinned at the woman who was engaged to his soon-to-be stepson. "We were hoping so. We'll talk later." He surveyed the table as though to say more but shook his head and sat back down. He kissed Nadine, who beamed at him.

"Did you know?" Maxwell whispered to Eryn.

"Dad told me last night," she whispered back. "I knew things were progressing this way already, so it wasn't a huge shock. The only surprise is how quickly they're moving."

Compared to Maxwell's promise to take things slow until he was absolutely sure? He already was, but there was still something there. Eryn wasn't ready, even if she thought she was. Or was he hedging for a different reason?

His prayer list kept getting longer.

MAXWELL OPENED the door from the conference room and beckoned her in. "They're ready for you."

Eryn took a deep breath and smoothed her hands down her skirt. "I'm nervous."

"There's nothing to worry about. You're going to rock this. I've got your presentation queued up. Ready?"

Was she? She'd worked so hard on ideas to turn that little gift shop into something the resort could be proud of, and here was her opportunity to have the Sullivan Enterprises board give her a chance to implement it. But she didn't want Nadine to think she was ungrateful for the job in the kitchen. It had been such a different dynamic than restaurant cooking, plus it had given her a chance to get to know Dad's girlfriend — now fiancée — on her own.

She looked up at Maxwell and nodded, quelling her churning gut.

He smiled, ushered her in, and indicated her place at the foot of the conference table. He sat around the corner and picked up the remote. "Ready?"

Eryn pulled back her shoulders and nodded as she met Walter Sullivan's gaze down the length of the table. "I'm sure Maxwell has already told you about my interest in the gift shop in the lobby. He encouraged me to create a proposal for what I feel the space could become."

He flicked a switch, and a 3D rotating rendering of the space appeared on the screen. It was certainly helpful having a boyfriend adept at CAD programs.

"I've contacted several local artisans who are interested in selling their wares through our gift shop."

Maxwell grinned at her, and she realized she'd called it *our* gift shop. Well, yes. After the course of the past six weeks, she'd come to think of it with ownership.

"We've already had pottery from Bayside Kiln on

display. Upon our go-ahead, Trinity will create a line of coffee mugs specifically for sale here. That's a pretty big deal because, as you know, she's mostly blind. But she has done some experimenting, and we feel we have a winning design."

Maxwell popped the rendering onto the screen to the murmur of approval from around the table.

Eryn gathered confidence from that and went on to describe and display the wares of the other vendors she'd contacted. She showed a mockup of jigsaw puzzles created from some of Cadence's photos as well as updates to the book rack as Maxwell's AI-generated walk-through followed along.

Then she lifted the table runner she'd pieced together night before last. She'd finally given in and pulled the bin with her favorite fabrics out, even though she and Dad were moving in a few days.

Maxwell's head tipped to the side, and he studied the runner. Did he not like it after he'd encouraged her to follow through? She had no time to worry about that now.

"Bravo!" Maribel clapped. "I love everything. I love the idea of our guests being able to purchase unique, locally made gifts and mementoes from our shop."

Maxwell's smirk wasn't missed by Eryn. He'd told her how adamantly against the purchase of the ranch his mother had been at first.

"Hear, hear!" Bridget nodded.

"Well done," James — Maxwell's dad — said.

"Any questions?" Eryn couldn't believe it had been that easy to win them all over. Though Maxwell had been right.

Anything would be better than the way the little space had been so neglected.

No. She straightened her shoulders. This was a thousand times better. This was *her* vision, and she was proud of the work she'd done to curate and fine-tune it.

Walter asked a few questions about sourcing. Graham was concerned about markups. Weston offered to create a prototype for braided-leather key fobs. Cool. She hadn't thought of something like that!

"One final question, Eryn," Walter said at last.

She steeled herself. "Yes, sir?"

"Is management of this gift shop something you would personally like to take on?"

Her gaze flicked to Nadine. The older woman smiled. "I've never managed a store before, so I'm not sure I have the skills."

"But would you like to?" Walter persisted.

Eryn took a deep breath. "Yes, sir, I'd like to try."

He waved a hand. "It's different here than retail elsewhere. You won't have to worry about payroll, since the ranch accounting department will handle that."

Graham nodded and keyed into his tablet.

"You also won't need to be concerned about utility bills or details like that." Walter held up a hand. "That's not to say the gift shop shouldn't be profitable, because it should. Every part of this operation needs to pay its own way plus at least a little extra."

Maxwell covered his smirk with his hand as he turned away from his grandfather.

The old man glanced around the table. "Does anyone have any objections to offering Eryn the opportunity to run with her plan? Not that I care what you all think. I still hold the reins around here." He gave a pointed look between his two sons.

Murmuring assent flowed from around the table.

He tapped a gavel lightly onto the table. Where had that thing come from, anyway? "Make a note of that in the records, Theodore."

"Yes, Father."

"Now, is there any other business we need to wrap up before our next meeting in April?"

By the shaking heads, that would be a no.

"Thank you." He looked at Eryn. "I look forward to seeing this become reality. Feel free to contact me directly if you need anything specific. Otherwise, I expect to see the room stocked and ready for business by the first of May. Is that doable?"

"Yes, sir." She'd heard that Memorial Day was the real kickoff for the resort, but she could have everything in place earlier. She was sure of it.

He gave a firm nod and closed his laptop. Others gathered up their notes as they chatted with each other.

Maxwell, who'd already turned off the presentation, stood and reached for her hand. "Come on. I've got something I want to show you."

"You do?" What could it be? He wasn't going to propose with a lead-in like that, was he?

They grabbed their jackets from near the front door, and he led her out to one of the little golf carts. They'd get parked when there was too much snow on the roads, but for now, they remained viable.

"Where are we going?"

"My place."

In the nearly two months she'd lived at Sweet River, she hadn't been inside Maxwell's home. With the attraction zinging between them, it hadn't seemed wise. Why now?

He pulled to a stop beside his duplex and ushered her inside. No surprise the place was perfectly tidy with a large desk holding three monitors taking up the place where the Ralstons' unit had a kitchen table.

"I want to show you the quilt I found in that attic three years ago."

"Okay?"

"Because I realized something interesting about it. Now, it might be a coincidence. It probably is, but maybe not."

"Something interesting?" She trailed him to the bedroom door.

He strode in and unfolded the quilt lying across the foot of the bed. The quilt...

Eryn gasped.

Maxwell shook it out and held it up. "Some of the fabric is the same as in the prototype for the table runners."

"I... I don't know what to say."

He laughed. "Did you make my quilt?"

"Wow." She shook her head. "I sewed that for a woman who ordered a custom quilt from the fabric store in Gilead. She wanted it for her mother-in-law in Chicago. That was five or six years ago."

"I've been snuggling with your quilt for four years. I can't believe it."

"I can't, either. What a crazy coincidence." Eryn traced her fingertip down the tiny stitches. "I only sewed the patchwork top, then Zoey hired someone with a quilting machine to finish it up. And it was stashed in the attic of a house you flipped?"

"Along with several other quilts and a whole raft of other things. The house owner had died suddenly, and her family just wanted rid of everything in one go, after they'd taken the heirlooms they wanted, I guess."

"It looks as good as new."

His eyes crinkled. "I've taken good care of it."

She laughed but couldn't take her eyes off the quilt. "I always loved this one. I doubt I can get the exact fabrics for the table runners — I just whipped that up with scraps I had left over. I'll need to go shopping."

"Whipped that up?" Maxwell laughed.

"Hey, you just 'whipped up' a mosaic design for the broken tile in that bathroom." He'd finally shown her around the cottages on Ladybug Lane the other day.

"That's true. And it looks pretty good, if I do say so myself."

"I'll say it for you, if needed."

"You know what looks good? You do. You *rocked* that presentation."

"I couldn't have without your help. The graphics helped a ton."

"It was all you, sweetie. That was just the cherry on top." Maxwell gathered her in his arms and kissed her tenderly.

No, his love was the cherry on top.

CHAPTER TWENTY-SEVEN

Maxwell adjusted his bow tie and smoothed the scarlet cummerbund. He'd once called it red, and Paisley had corrected him. He'd been more careful after that. He studied himself in the full-length mirror and flicked what might have been a piece of lint off his tuxedo's black sleeve.

Someone tapped at the door, and he turned toward it. "Yes?"

It opened, and Weston and Jude entered, wearing tuxes similar to his. Weston tugged at his tie. "How do you get used to being choked?"

"Choked?" Maxwell laughed and crossed the space. "Let me adjust that thing for you. Paisley tightened it right up?"

Jude snickered. "She's making sure you remember who's boss."

Weston sneered at his brother. "You're just jealous."

And Jude actually shut up and turned away. Huh.

"You guys ready?" Maxwell looked between the Kline brothers.

"I guess."

"Consider it a dress rehearsal for your own wedding. That's, what, only three months away?"

Weston let out a long breath. "Is that all? I mean, how time drags."

Maxwell knew what Weston meant. Time was such a weird thing, appearing to speed and linger at the same time. He could hardly believe it had been three months since he'd reconnected with Eryn. She'd come so far — they both had, actually. But she was so much more confident now. It was wondrous and beautiful to see.

Jude checked his watch. "I think we're supposed to be downstairs in like zero minutes."

"Is Nana ready?" Weston asked.

Jude nodded. "She was so tickled Mom asked her to stand up with her."

"What an interesting wedding party." Maxwell laughed. Keith and Nadine had asked their three kids, then immediately included Maxwell and Paisley. Jude would be paired with his grandmother, but he claimed to be honored rather than insulted.

"Let's do it." Weston brushed his hands together. "The sooner we get them hitched, the sooner I can get back in jeans and a Henley."

"After all the photos and the reception." Maxwell couldn't help goading his cousin. It was simply too much fun.

"I'll talk to Paisley again about eloping. Why does she have to be an event planner, anyway? I can't believe how extravagant she's making everything."

"But you're getting married here, at the ranch..." How extravagant could it be?

Weston mock shuddered.

"Time." Jude pointed at the door. "Let's not be the ones holding up the show."

Maxwell followed his cousins down the back stairs to the office hallway, where Pastor Marshall Smith from Creekside Fellowship met them. "You boys ready?"

They nodded just as Keith joined them from a side room. The groom looked like he'd been born to a tux instead of to overalls, and the smile on his face could not be contained. He looked around the group. "Is everything running on time?"

"Paisley would have our heads if it wasn't," Weston muttered.

Maxwell tried not to smirk, but the truth was, he couldn't wait for a glimpse of Eryn in her scarlet — not red — gown. Weston might be alternating cold and eager feet, but Maxwell had yet to pop his own question and formalize his relationship with Eryn. Oh, they'd talked about marriage and kids and the pros and cons of living at the ranch versus in town, but always in a hypothetical sense.

Cadence poked her head around to see the men. "I was sent to tell you to make your entrance now."

Keith nodded and pumped his shoulders. "Let's do this." He followed Pastor Smith down the corridor, the younger men behind him, Maxwell sandwiched between Weston and Jude.

The great room had been mounded with greenery and

assorted white flowers to offset the bank of leftover Christmas poinsettias, the perfume of them filling the air. Guests, including Maxwell's parents and aunt and uncle, sat in rows of folding chairs facing the crackling fireplace and the wide windows with their lake view.

Maxwell faced the gathering, but his gaze strayed beyond to the grand log staircase from the second floor. The string quartet's selection shifted, and Eleanor began her descent of the steps. She might be 77, but she was steady on her feet and elegant in her gown. Jude met her and ushered her to her spot.

Then it was Paisley's turn. A quick glance to Weston showed the surly cowboy spellbound, his mouth slightly agape as he watched his fiancée.

Maxwell elbowed him lightly and whispered, "Maybe the hoopla is worth it?"

"Maybe," Weston whispered back then stepped forward to escort her.

And then Eryn stepped into view, and Maxwell forgot to breathe. She was so beautiful in that gorgeous dress. Her hair, like Paisley's, was in an updo with a few trailing tendrils framing her face. Eryn's gaze latched onto his, and he couldn't have stayed standing where he was if his life depended on it.

Thankfully, it didn't. Thankfully, he'd been ordered to meet her, and he did. She tucked her hand behind his elbow and pressed against him.

"You're stunning," he whispered.

"You clean up pretty well yourself," she whispered back.

Maxwell's mother glowered at him as they passed her

seat, but whatever. He was going to flirt with his girlfriend at her father's wedding if he wanted to.

All too soon, he left her and crossed to stand in his own assigned spot.

The wedding march began, and Grandfather and Nadine appeared at the top of the stairs. Nadine had opted for a pastel pink gown that coordinated with the other dresses, or so Eryn had explained.

Grandfather had insisted on giving his daughter away, saying he'd missed far too much in her life, including her first wedding. He was going to do it right this time. Part of *doing it right* seemed to be the flower shop that appeared to have exploded all over the lodge.

Pastor Smith began the ceremony, and Maxwell did his best to focus. He'd paid little attention during Tate's wedding to Stephanie or during Graham's wedding to Cadence. It was different today, knowing Eryn. Loving her. Wanting to spend the rest of his life making her happy. Making her his.

Were all wedding sermons based on First Corinthians 13? Maybe Maxwell should ask Pastor Smith if he had another variation. Or would they ask Eli Bryson to marry them? His gaze drifted to Eryn, who appeared to be intent on the officiant.

Focus, Maxwell. Focus.

It seemed no time at all before Keith and Nadine were presented as man and wife and were kissing like teenagers. Good to know passion could still exist in one's fifties.

There'd be photos and the reception and the dance and then the newlyweds would head for their Hawaiian honeymoon. That chapter would close, and Maxwell would turn the page to a new one.

ERYN SIGHED against Maxwell as the final notes of music faded away. They stood at the edge of the dance floor, holding each other close. She could feel his heartbeat against her cheek.

She'd never felt safer. More loved. It had been days — weeks, maybe — since she'd thought much about Amelia. Now she was sorry for her sister's bitterness. Sorry Amelia couldn't have been present to see how happy their father was with his new love, his new life. Oh, he'd loved Mom, no doubt about it, but he'd gratefully received a second shot at happiness.

"How are you doing?" Maxwell murmured against her hair. "It's been a busy day."

"It has." She exhaled. "Good, though. I'm glad Dad's so happy." He and Nadine had headed off not 20 minutes back.

"And you're moving back into the duplexes."

Eryn chuckled. "It was nice living in the farmhouse while it lasted, but the newlyweds need their space. Besides, it's time I left the nest, don't you think?"

"I definitely agree." Maxwell's hands splayed across her back, pressing her against him.

He seemed to be drifting away from the thinning crowd, but she didn't care. A quieter place to unwind one-on-one would be welcome. But he fumbled with a door-knob behind him and pulled her through, into...

The gift shop? They'd been working in here lately, painting the space and updating the flooring. Jordan was building new shelves, and Eryn had begun ordering stock for the grand reopening in four months.

Now the room was bathed in fairy lights, and soft music played. A bank of flowers filled the area where the pottery display would be, its heady perfume permeating the space.

"This is beautiful." Eryn looked up at Maxwell, only he wasn't there, but kneeling before her. She gasped, and her hand covered her mouth.

"Eryn Ann Ralston, I love you with everything in my being. You've changed everything about my life in the best possible way. You've challenged me to grow closer to God, and you've suffused my life with happiness and hope. Would you please do me the honor of becoming my wife? I want to spend the rest of my life beside you, honoring you and loving you."

He held a ring box toward her. A diamond flanked by two garnets winked up at her.

Was this real? Had her moment finally come? She reached a tentative finger to touch the diamond. It certainly felt solid.

Eryn dropped to her knees in front of Maxwell and grasped both his hands in hers, the little ring box at the center. "Is this a promise?"

He gazed into her eyes, the expression in his brown ones softening. "It's more than a promise, my love. It's a pact, a marriage pact. I pledge my love to you as long as we both shall live."

"Isn't that what you say during the wedding?"

"I'll say it again then. I'll say it to you as often as you need to hear it." He stretched across and brushed his lips against hers, his gaze still intent. "But more than that, I pledge to live it."

"Maxwell... I don't even know your middle name."

"Jefferson."

She blinked. "Seriously?"

"Seriously." He chuckled.

"Maxwell Jefferson Sullivan, I accept your proposal and your pledge. I love you more than I ever thought possible, and I can't think of anything better than spending the rest of my life at your side."

He tugged the ring from its velvet nest and slipped it onto her finger. Then he lifted Eryn to her feet and twirled her around. She clung to his shoulders as they spun.

When he finally set her down, she took his beloved face between her hands and looked deeply into his eyes. "I love you, Maxwell. I'll do my best to be worthy of you."

He shook his head slowly. "You *are* worthy. You don't need to try. Just be yourself. If we keep close to God, keep our focus on Him and then each other, we'll be okay."

"We need to fill our minds with His word. With positive things." Not dwell on negatives like she'd been so prone to doing.

From back in the great room, an air horn sounded. "Ten, nine, eight..."

"I love you, Eryn."

It was a good thing he'd said her name, because when his lips brushed hers again, she all but forgot who she was. The sweet, tender caress slowly deepened until Eryn was lost in this moment with her beloved.

The air horn blasted again, long and loud.

"Happy New Year, Eryn," Maxwell whispered into the sudden silence.

"Happy New Year, Maxwell."

She was going to marry her greatest love and pledge her life to his in this most precious of new years.

Cheers, whistles, and cat calls came from the great room.

They'd figure out the details later.

EPILOGUE

Bryce Sullivan stood beside the fireplace, watching the crowd mill around the lodge's great room. Aunt Nadine had married Keith Ralston an hour or so ago, and the party was still in full swing. His gaze caught on a redhead, standing with her back to him, across the room.

His heart stopped abruptly. What on earth was Madison Woodrow doing in Montana, at Bryce's aunt's wedding?

He edged around the crowd, drawn, as always, to her like a magnet. What was he going to say when he got her attention? It wasn't like he wanted to rekindle anything with her. She'd leave after the reception, right? He didn't need to say anything at all.

She'd cut her hair by a few inches and curled it. Maybe lightened it a little, but why would she do that? She'd always been so proud of the natural red and made sure people knew the color wasn't out of a bottle.

The woman turned, her gaze meeting Bryce's from a few feet away. She smiled.

She was not Madison.

That was good, right? He could breathe again. Because Madison didn't belong in Montana. She was a Chicago girl. She didn't belong with Bryce's family.

The woman held eye contact as she said something to her companion. Now two women were smiling and watching him.

"Hey, there. I'm Bryce. Nadine's nephew." He stuck out his hand. "I didn't mean to stare. It's just you reminded me of someone I used to know."

"Or someone you want to know, maybe? I'm Daniella Evans, Reggie's daughter."

Reggie was Aunt Nadine's stepbrother. Relief swarmed Bryce. "We're practically cousins."

Daniella touched his arm. "But not quite. There's no blood between us." She waggled her eyebrows.

She offered the kind of invitation the old Bryce would have gone for, but nope. Not with someone who reminded him of Madison. Not with someone who was practically related. That would just get messy, since Bryce wasn't into commitment.

Ask Madison about that.

Or not.

She'd pushed him so hard after their breakup that he'd felt nothing but relief when Grandfather summoned him to Montana. She'd seemed unable to take no for an answer. Bryce had no illusions that he was a great catch. Sure, the Sullivans had a pile of money, but the Woodrows weren't exactly paupers. Madison didn't need him that way.

Man, she'd been persistent.

The two women giggled.

Bryce remembered where he was. He took a step back. "It was nice meeting you, Daniella." He nodded to the other woman before pivoting and heading for the buffet.

Whew. Close call.

He loaded his plate with food he wasn't hungry for and retreated to his spot by the fireplace. Look at him. Since when was Bryce the guy on the edges?

With Eleanor on his arm, Grandfather made the rounds of the room, chatting with their guests. Maybe Bryce should shift elsewhere and avoid the old man. But why? He hadn't done anything wrong.

Not lately, anyway.

Much.

"Happy New Year, Bryce!" Grandfather saluted him with a goblet of grape juice. Not even wine.

"Happy New Year, sir." Bryce nodded at Nadine's mother. "And you, Eleanor." Would the elderly pair marry in the coming year? By the smiles both wore, Bryce wouldn't be shocked to hear of it.

"What are your hopes and plans for the upcoming year, Bryce?" Grandfather inquired.

What kind of question was that? Bryce stared at the man. "Uh… the usual, I guess. All the landscaping around this ranch that your heart could desire. Maxwell and I were designing the grounds around the new treehouses the other day."

"Any personal plans?"

Bryce blinked. "Not really, sir."

Grandfather nodded and looked at the flames flickering

in the fireplace. "Well, keep an open mind, boy, and pray about it. You never know what will happen."

Maybe Dad and Uncle Theodore were right in thinking the old man was off his rocker, though he usually seemed sharp enough.

Like now. Grandfather turned back and held Bryce's gaze for a long moment, seemingly waiting for a response.

"Uh, yes, sir. I'll do that." At least the open mind, part. Hey, it could happen. They'd have a new crop of seasonal employees starting in May. Maybe there'd be some amazing woman who could drive Madison out of Bryce's memories.

He could only hope.

As for praying, fat chance. He'd attended Sunday school as a kid in Kansas, of course, plus he'd attended at least a dozen iterations of the passion play over the years. He knew the basics. But how could it be relevant?

God was a bandaid. A crutch. Bryce didn't need that. He was doing just fine on his own.

Sort of fine.

Not so fine.

Ugh.

A NOTE...

Dear Bryce,

You're going to be a challenge, aren't you? Readers don't even like you right now. I'm not sure I do, either.

I'm trusting the Lord to give me your story and to make it one that will draw my readers and me closer to the Lord. And you, as well, if it's not too weird to pray for fictional people.

Okay, that IS weird, but I can't help it. See you soon!

Your loving author, Valerie

Dear Reader,

I hope you loved Eryn and Maxwell! Like me, you were probably wishing Eryn would just STOP reading her sister's journals already, but I hope you understood what a vital part of her growth that hangup became. I loved Maxwell as he learned to step back and be patient!

And then there was Bryce, continuously interfering where he wasn't wanted! But he's next on the redemption schedule. I mean, writing schedule!

You can order Bryce's and Madison's story, A Secret Baby for the Cowboy, today!

I look forward to meeting you again soon in the log lodge at Sweet River Ranch.

Blessings, Valerie

Psst: Reviews are awesome, too…

ACKNOWLEDGMENTS

Thank you, dear reader, for loving all of the Montana Ranches Christian Romance series: Saddle Springs, Cavanagh Cowboys, and now Sweet River! I'm excited to write the stories of the remaining Sullivan grandsons in the next few months.

Thanks to my author buddies Elizabeth Maddrey, Lynnette Bonner, and Jan Thompson for writing sprints and accountability. Friends make such a difference.

My amazing editor, Nicole, has been with me from the beginning. I am so thankful for her!

I'm also grateful for the Christian Indie Authors Facebook group. These folks make a difference in my life every single day. I'm thrilled to walk beside them as we tell stories for Jesus!

Thank you to my Facebook friends, followers, street team, and reader group members for prayers, encouragement, and great fellowship. If you'd like to join other readers who love my stories, please find us at Valerie Comer: Readers Group.

Thanks to my husband, Jim, whose love for me never fails and who encourages me in every endeavor. Thanks to my kids, their spouses, and my wonderful grandkids for cheering me on. To them, having an author for a mom/grandma is "normal." Imagine that!

All my love and gratitude goes to Jesus, the One who is my vision, the High King of Heaven, the lord of my heart. Thank You. A thousand times, thank You.

DEAR READER...

Thanks for reading *A Marriage Pact for the Cowboy*! I'm so honored that you chose to spend the last few hours with Maxwell, Eryn, and me. You are appreciated.

I'm an independent author who relies on my readers to help spread the word about stories you enjoy. Would you take a few minutes to let your friends know? Facebook, Instagram, Goodreads... wherever you hang out online.

Also, each honest review at online retailers means a lot to me and helps other readers know if this is a book they might enjoy. I'd sure appreciate your help getting word out!

I welcome contact from readers. At my website, you can contact me via email, read my blog, and find me on social media. You can also sign up for my newsletter to be notified of new releases, contests, special deals, and more! Click here to subscribe. You'll receive *The Cowboy's Forever Crush*, the novella that introduces all of my Montana Ranches Christian Romance series, absolutely free as my thank you gift!

~ Valerie Comer

www.valeriecomer.com

https://valeriecomer.com/subscribe-crush

BOOKS BY VALERIE COMER

You'll find the complete list of titles by Valerie Comer on her website: fifty books (and counting) in ten series! Come on over to find farm-fresh romance, cowboy romance, and small-town romance, all with distinctly Christian themes.

https://valeriecomer.com/books

ABOUT VALERIE COMER

Valerie Comer is constantly amazed that living, talking, dreaming characters appear in her mind and flow from her fingertips and, from there, to her delighted readers. She only hopes her creations enjoy their happily-ever-afters as much as she does hers, sharing rural life in western Canada with her husband, adult children, and adorable grandkids.

Valerie is a two-time *USA Today* bestselling author and a two-time Word Award winner. She is known for writing engaging characters, strong communities, and deep faith into her green clean romances.

To find out more, visit her website at www.valeriecomer.com, where you can read her blog, explore her many links, and sign up for her email newsletter, where you will find news, giveaways, deals, book recommendations and more. You can also find Valerie blogging with other authors of Christian contemporary romance at Inspy Romance.